Christmas in Kissinger

by

Misty Simon

Kissinger Kisses, Book Four

This is a work of fiction. Names, characters, places, and incidents are either the product of the author's imagination or are used fictitiously, and any resemblance to actual persons living or dead, business establishments, events, or locales, is entirely coincidental.

Christmas in Kissinger

Cover Art by *Debbie Taylor*

The Wild Rose Press, Inc.
PO Box 708
Adams Basin, NY 14410-0708
Visit us at www.thewildrosepress.com

Publishing History
First Champagne Rose Edition, 2016
Print ISBN 978-1-5092-0960-6
Digital ISBN 978-1-5092-0961-3

Kissinger Kisses, Book Four
Published in the United States of America

Jocelyn had no problem with teaching the guys a special dance for the wedding. She thought it was beyond adorable that he had even thought of it. But if Flo was going to try to play matchmaker, then life was going to be rough for the next week.

Music started in the room she'd named "Pas de chat," the one she'd set up for the guys. A waltz threaded through the air, and Jocelyn stopped tutu duty long enough to check out what they'd be working with.

Exiting the back room, she looked at her clipboard one more time to make sure she was only waiting for one more set of boxes. She was pleased to find her calculations were right. Not so pleased when someone rammed into her, then swept her off her feet.

"Hey!" she said as she registered the big forearm against her back and the other behind her knees. A scent tickled her nose with memories long buried.

She looked up into the velvetiest brown eyes imaginable. They crinkled at the corners in a way they hadn't eleven years ago, with lines fanning out from the sides that were either from laughing or frowning.

At the moment they were laughing, and she was not amused even if she was shocked enough to not immediately demand to be put down.

Dedication

To all the readers who've been on this journey with me…Let's get the rest of them happily paired off!

Absolutely No Returns or Exchanges

by

Misty Simon

Misty Simon

Chapter One

Another day, another delivery of tutus. Jocelyn Moreland slowly slid a box cutter through the tape holding the enormous box of fluff closed. If she wasn't careful, she'd have another Mount Vesuvius-sized eruption of tulle, like yesterday.

"Jocelyn, remember we have the first class for that wedding in an hour." Five feet nothing of pluck and gumption, Jocelyn's mother, Flo Caster, came steaming into the room with a huge smile on her face.

"Of course I remember." They had three weeks until the holiday recital, and she really shouldn't have taken on anything else. But when your best friend's fiancé asks for dancing lessons to impress his future bride, you don't turn them down. Somehow this would all work out. "I hope Zoe appreciates what the guys are doing."

"She'll be delighted. Who wouldn't? It's so cute that he wants to surprise her." Flo stood with her hands on her hips. "It's romantic, too. Maybe he should start giving lessons of his own. Everyone needs a little romance in their lives." She eyed Jocelyn from head to toe. "You could stand for some yourself, missy."

As always, Jocelyn ignored her when she tried to talk guys or romance or love or any of that other sappy crap. "I think it'll be fun. I don't know how I'm going to keep it a secret from her, though, or how the guys

3

will, for that matter."

"They'll figure it out. And just you watch—it will be magnificent. The secret isn't going to be hard to keep. Besides it's only for a week. Just don't say anything."

"Ha! That might be easier said than done."

"You'll manage. You've kept secrets before."

Because she didn't want to have that particular conversation again, Jocelyn headed her mother off for a second time. "Do you need anything before the guys get here? Are you ready?" The woman was her staunchest support while also being the cause of most of her headaches. She wouldn't trade her for the world, though.

"Of course I'm absolutely ready. I might need you in there with all that testosterone, though." She laughed, then threw Jocelyn a sly look. "Hey, now, maybe we can get you hooked up with one of them." Flo tapped her chin with a long index finger. "Surely they're not all taken already." Flo's cheeky smile was enough to make Jocelyn sigh and cringe at the same time. It was a continuous struggle when she wanted both to laugh at the fact that her mother never stopped and to scream that her mother never stopped. Tenacity should have been her middle name instead of Anna.

Plopping both hands on her hips, Jocelyn opened her mouth with every intention of telling her mom that whatever scheme she had in her brain was not going to fly. Before she could get a single word out, she watched in horror as the whole line of tape on the box cracked, followed closely by the rush of tutus thrust into the air as if trying to escape a maximum security prison.

She got a faceful of tulle as she tried to shepherd

them all back into the box. "We're not doing this, Mom. You're going to be the death of me. Remember your last set-up? Because I do. Vividly. In my nightmares."

Flo scoffed. "You're exaggerating. It wasn't that bad."

That finally got Jocelyn to laugh out loud. "Wasn't that bad? Perhaps in comparison to being eaten alive by a boa constrictor, but it wasn't exactly good, and you know it."

"Well, with that attitude, of course it wasn't good. You have to overlook some things to get to the good stuff." Flo's face crinkled up, her back going ramrod straight.

Jocelyn would have to head her off before she had convinced herself that she should set up a second date for Jocelyn with Roger the tarantula wrangler. "Let's concentrate on now. You have a man class to get ready for, and I have to get these tutus situated on hangers."

Keeping her hand and most of her weight on the top of the box, Jocelyn tried to ignore the mischief shining on Flo's face.

"Don't flirt with any of them yourself, either," Jocelyn said.

"Oh, come on, now, you're no fun. I can flirt with whoever I want to. I'm not married to your stepfather anymore, and I'm not dead. Besides, it's all part of the service, and if it makes some of them want to sign up for additional classtime here, then so much the better. And if they flirt back, then so much the better. Think about what a coup that would be, to have an adult class with men in it. We could be bigger than even you imagined when you bought the studio from Beulah two years ago."

Jocelyn groaned and slapped her free hand to her forehead. "Seriously, Mother, you're killing me. Go get dressed. I have a class in an hour and a half and about two hundred replacement tutus to hang in the meantime." She'd sent them all back the first time because the stitching was not right. She might not run a big city studio, but she did run a tight and professional ship when it came to the quality provided.

On a laugh, Flo jetéd out of the back room, her body as spry as a teenager's as she leapt and landed. Jocelyn shook her head. The woman was almost sixty and completely unstoppable. Jocelyn hoped to be like her when she grew up.

An hour later, heavy footsteps sounded in the foyer. The guys were here. Jocelyn smiled to herself as she put another tutu on a plastic hanger and placed it on the rolling dressing room rack. Dexter Zegray had first approached her at a Halloween party a month ago to ask if she could point him in the right direction for ballroom lessons. She'd hesitated to offer Flo, but the lady herself, dressed like a flapper from the twenties, had swooped in with her fake cigarette and her on-display garters and had immediately signed him up.

Of course, Jocelyn had no problem with teaching the guys a special dance for the wedding. She thought it was beyond adorable that he had even thought of it. But if Flo was going to try to play matchmaker, then life was going to be rough for the next week.

Music started in the room she'd named "Pas de chat," the one she'd set up for the guys. A waltz threaded through the air, and Jocelyn stopped tutu duty long enough to check out what they'd be working with.

Exiting the back room, she looked at her clipboard one more time to make sure she was only waiting for one more set of boxes. She was pleased to find her calculations were right. Not so pleased when someone rammed into her, then swept her off her feet.

"Hey!" she said as she registered the big forearm against her back and the other behind her knees. A scent tickled her nose with memories long buried.

She looked up into the velvetiest brown eyes imaginable. They crinkled at the corners in a way they hadn't eleven years ago, with lines fanning out from the sides that were either from laughing or frowning.

At the moment they were laughing, and she was not amused even if she was shocked enough to not immediately demand to be put down.

****

Sam Locke hadn't had an armful this amazing in more than a decade, and he didn't want to put her down now. He knew he should. He could see from the thunderclouds brewing on her expressive face that he was about to be blasted with thunder like he hadn't heard in years. Yet it would be worth it to hold her curves for just another moment or two.

In the end, she squirmed to the point that not only was he having a bodily reaction—which could be embarrassing while he was learning this dance—but he was about to drop her.

He set her on her feet, then stepped back when she crossed her arms hard over her chest. She was rounder than he remembered, but she'd filled out in ways that couldn't have pleased him more. God, it was good to see her.

"Well, if it isn't Jocelyn Locke."

"It's Moreland now." She kept those arms locked hard, unintentionally plumping some of her more obvious attributes.

"You went back to your maiden name, huh?" Something pinged under his breastbone, but he knew he had no say in the matter. Hadn't for years.

"Yes."

They stared at each other for a few moments as the reality of the situation settled in. The instantaneous joy of seeing her again faded, replaced as memories of the end of their relationship surged forward. His smile dimmed, the muscles moving down as she continued to scowl at him.

"Why are you here?" she asked, eyeing him up and down.

He fought the urge to tug on his T-shirt and shake out his jeans. He'd come straight from the shop, knowing he was going to be late and also knowing that he wasn't here to impress anyone. Dex had said their teacher was a middle-aged fun lady who'd been a professional dancer back in the day. He'd expected a retired ballroom dancer or a ballerina. Because he knew his stuff, and the studio was less than twenty minutes from his house, he'd worked longer than he probably should have and come straight here from his metal shop. He had a ton of work to do and little time to spare. But he was willing to give some of it up to make Dex and Zoe happy. They'd come through a pretty rough patch a few months ago. He was glad their family was intact and that he'd gotten his apprentice back.

He brought himself out of his mental meandering to answer her question. "I have lessons."

"You what?" Her mouth hung open. He wanted to

put his hand under her chin to close it. Really, any excuse to touch her again.

But he kept his hands and his thoughts to himself.

He gestured to the room with four guys trying out some stretches and looking like mannequins in a store window. "I'm here for that thing with Dex. He wants us to learn dances for his wedding. So here I am, ready to learn dances." He spread his arms wide and gave her his best smile.

A frown dragged down her mouth to mimic the way her brow furrowed with her scowl. "You are not here to dance."

She declared it. There was no question.

He stood straighter and let go of the hem of his T-shirt, crossing his own arms. "I most certainly am here to dance."

"You can't be."

"And yet somehow I am. What's wrong with that?"

"But, but, but… This is my studio." Her incredulity was something to behold. Surely it wasn't the end of the world that he was here in her sacred studio.

"Okay. And what? I can't be a customer because you own it? It's been eleven years. I'm sure Dex paid you well enough even to teach scum like me." He widened his stance and stared her down.

"Oh!" Her breath caught in her pretty throat. "You are a jackass," she hissed.

"Thanks, sweetheart." He patted her cheek, knowing full well it would irritate the shit out of her. Well, she could join the party. "Now if you could point me in the direction of my teacher?"

"Sam!" a feminine voice called out to him from down the hall.

He turned just his head and zeroed in on a woman who probably came up to his bottom rib. She beckoned him with a hand and a smile.

"Come on in. We're just getting started."

He turned back to Jocelyn, smirked at her (which probably was not his smartest idea ever), and then loosened his arms and sauntered away from the one woman he had never been able to get over, no matter how many years and how many women in between.

****

"That jackass. Jackass!" Jocelyn paced in the storage room at the back of the studio. She had five minutes until she had to start her preschool class, and she felt like an enormous elephant was sitting in her way. Not that Sam Locke was an elephant. God, no. He was still tall, still built. But now he had a man's body, solid, strong, beautiful. If he had been anyone else, she would have been drooling all over him.

But he wasn't just anyone. He was her freaking ex-husband. Which put her back to the elephant thing.

She had two minutes until class and a roomful of four-year-olds who expected her to be Happy Miss Jocelyn, not Brooding Mean Bitch.

Okay, she could do this.

Stepping out from the back room, she smoothed down her jazz pants, made sure her hair was still in its ponytail, and prepared to face twenty girls who were here to have a good time while learning grace at the same time. She wasn't prepared for their moms.

"Oh, my word, Miss Jocelyn."

The sentiment echoed throughout the waiting room. All the mothers in attendance stood riveted by the glass window that perfectly showcased five men trying valiantly to follow Flo's steps. Only one was catching on quickly, but she avoided giving him even a second of her notice. Flo, of course, touched a little too frequently, straightening this one's leg and making that one tuck his rear end in.

Jocelyn would have slapped a hand over her eyes, but she had drooling women behind her and soon-to-be-restless kids.

"Are we ready to dance?" she asked in her teacher voice, part sing-song, part stern, but all fun. At least she could still make that work.

"Can I join that class?" Heather Manchester asked, pointing at the guys.

Jocelyn forced a laugh. "No, but they'll be here for seven days, so you can watch without joining."

"Ohhhhh." The collective sigh was enough to make Jocelyn itchy.

Please save her from preschool moms who came to dance class to get out of the house and gossip. Apparently they had no issue with ogling strange men, either. She'd add it to her list of provided activities.

Without another moment's hesitation, she ushered the little girls into the classroom next to the guys. No one was actually going to watch their little munchkin dance this afternoon. They'd all be gawking at the fine male specimens next door. Let them ogle. She was happy to have people dancing in her studio at all.

It had been a close thing at first, she thought as she started up the music and let the student aides lead the four-year-olds through their stretches. She'd bought the studio from the previous owner, one Beulah Jameson, who was strict and kind but still really strict. Jocelyn had taken what Beulah had built over fifty years and had put a modern twist on it, adding new and different classes, taking the emphasis off perfection and the aim of getting the girls into prestigious dancing schools. Instead she focused on making it fun. She took anyone who had a desire to dance, not just the talent. After changing the name to Barre None, as a play on words, the last year had been much smoother sailing. Which, of course, meant she should have been ready for something like Sam to happen.

God, Sam. Those few moments in his arms had brought back so many memories that should have been left buried.

Stretch time was over, and Brittany Michaels was running around in circles and then smooshing her face up against the wall-length mirror.

"Okay, let's get started. Who remembers first position?"

She heard a burst of laughter next door and turned the stereo up with the remote control. She would survive the next week, even if it killed her.

Chapter Two

Sam had to remember to bring better socks next time. He'd known that any kind of dancing in work boots was totally out of the question, so he thought he'd been prepared. Flo had asked them to take their shoes off as soon as they'd come into the room. Protecting the expensive dance floors was rule number one at any good studio. But in his haste he'd run out with the socks he'd put on in the dark this morning. One had a hole in the toe and both had definitely seen better days.

As any instructor worth her salt would, Flo had recommended they all buy jazz shoes. Not surprisingly, her words were met with loud male laughter, followed by Dex threatening to buy them each a pair.

He wasn't going to get any of those girly shoes, but he could definitely make time to buy some new socks and probably dress better, too, if he was going to be seeing Jocelyn.

On the way out, he looked for her, wanting just one more glimpse of her before he left. That made him pathetic, but he didn't care. Flo had tortured them into dancing each part over and over again, going over the same four steps until they got it down without falling all over themselves, then moving on to the next four steps. He'd had no trouble picking it up, since it was pretty basic, but the other guys hadn't done so well. He hoped like hell Jack's wife had toes of steel when the wedding came.

Of course there'd be a lot more steps to add on in the next seven nights, but Flo had promised those would be repetitions of what they'd already done. Supposedly it would all make sense in the end when they put it all together. For the finale, they would all choose partners and do a waltz.

Given the choice, he'd pick the girl behind window one.

He stopped outside the room where Jocelyn bent at the waist and dropped her hand to the floor. Twenty little girls followed her lead with varying degrees of success. Ponytails flopped, skirts twitched, knees bent, but never Jocelyn's. She was straight and poised and beautiful.

Her head came up like she could sense he was watching her. She looked right at him, and he waved to her, just a tiny one so the other guys wouldn't notice. A second later that scowl was back on her face.

Probably not today, then. He had been thinking about hanging out to see if he could talk to her, but her body language was all but screaming that she did not want to be talked to. Sherlock, that was him. Could have had something to do with the fact that her every sentence had been stiff, her every expression completely lacking any friendliness. He had little doubt that if he'd been here by himself to take some lessons she would have handed him his money back right before kicking him out of the studio.

He'd have to thank Dex and find a way to do it without spilling his cards.

"So, uh, buddy." Dex held open the door to the parking lot and waited for Sam to go through before stepping out behind him.

"Yeah?"

"You already have a crush on the owner?" Dex hung a duffel bag on his shoulder like they were just coming out of the gym. It felt like it, to some extent, because that had been a serious workout. Leave it to Dex to always have the right accessories.

"No, not a crush. Just looking." Sam shrugged it off as if it were no big deal, when that couldn't be further from the truth.

"That looked like more than looking," Nate chimed in.

Like he needed to be doubled up on right now. He was still trying to come to terms with the fact that he'd just seen Jocelyn for the first time in eleven years. He didn't need an interrogation. Of course, there was one way to shut this whole thing down. He wasn't going to do it, though.

"Nah," he answered.

"You're lying." Dex crossed his arms over his chest. "Did you happen to forget that I'm a lawyer? I know a lie from a mile away, and you're standing close enough for me to sniff you. Now, out with it. You have a crush? Because I have to warn you she's friends with the ladies."

"I don't have a crush," he said, exasperation and a little desperation tingeing his voice.

"You have a crush!" Jack, from the inn, said. If Sam had expected anyone to be on his side he would have thought it would be Jack. Apparently not.

He was going to have to do it. There was a reason none of them knew this little part of his life. He hadn't wanted to rehash the past, especially when he'd thought he was over her and the small blip of time she'd filled in his life. He'd thought it wasn't important and would never be relevant to any conversation. But if they were going to be dancing here and she was friends with the women in their lives, then it was going to come out sooner or later.

"It's not a crush." He sighed as he ran a hand over the back of his head and neck. "We were married for about nine months. I haven't seen her in eleven years, and since I might see if I can change that, it's not a crush but an intention." Did he really mean that? He poked at it mentally and realized he did. He was either an idiot or a fool. He'd figure out which later, when he was by himself and could take the time to think this all the way through instead of being only a few feet away from her.

"What?" all four guys said in unison.

Sam enjoyed the moment. In fact he took their stunned silence as an opportunity to get in his truck and drive away.

His cell phone rang as soon as he cleared the driveway, but he wasn't going to answer it just yet. He needed a few moments to himself to digest what he'd just said. Yes, it had been good to see her, and to see her succeeding, but was he going to go after her for real?

He shouldn't. He really shouldn't. And yet he couldn't think of anything he'd like better…

Grabbing some dinner sounded like the best idea at the moment. Before his dance lesson, he'd sent his shop helper, Ethan, home. The guy had a new family and responsibilities. He wouldn't want to come back to get more work done. Sam didn't blame him one bit. But

Sam still had that option. With the shop out behind his house, he could work at all hours. With the swirl of shit going on inside him right now, that might be the best place for him.

****

One more class and then she was done for the night. Except she had forgotten she was supposed to go out with Zoe for coffee after their Zumba class. Damn. How was she going to keep her cool when she really wanted to confide in her friend? But how could she say something without unintentionally spilling the beans about him being at the studio? Which would lead to more questions that could let the dance cat out of the bag.

But she was almost positive Dex had said something to her friend. She'd seen the guys grouped together outside on the sidewalk, talking, and then Sam hightailing it out of her parking lot, leaving the other four men standing with their expressions shocked. What other news could he have shared but their failed marriage? So if Zoe knew, Jocelyn wasn't going to be able to get out of the conversation. In the end, she decided to let Zoe lead the way, if she asked at all.

The complications stacking up in her head made her temples throb.

Zoe kept trying to catch her eye during the whole class, making Jocelyn think Dex might have already said something to her. Lordy, what a talk that was going to be.

But not right now. Right now Jocelyn kept the ladies hopping. She had a weekly Zumba class for those who wanted some fun and exercise at the same time. Normally they laughed and talked between songs, but tonight she was being a taskmaster. And the ladies were sweating for it.

With a final flip of her hand and twitch of her hips, Jocelyn let the song wind down to nothing. The room reverberated with the huffing and puffing of fifteen gleaming women. "Okay, let's do a cool down."

"Whew!" Allison Michaelson said, swiping the brown hair off her forehead with the back of her hand. "I don't think I've ever danced so hard. Something got you moving tonight, Miss Jocelyn?"

Just like in most studios across the nation, all teachers were Miss something, and she was called Miss Jocelyn. She liked that, even for the adults, because it put a little distance between them. Then again, the way Zoe was eyeing her, even if she made her call her Miss Moreland she would still be grilling her in less than ten minutes.

"Just thought we'd get the blood going tonight," Jocelyn answered, not ashamed to admit that she'd worked them hard. They didn't perform in the recitals, but they were still here every week, and they paid her money to learn, to move, and she was giving that to them.

"Well, we certainly did that," Rose, a retired schoolteacher, said with a grin.

Everyone laughed and started into the stretch. Jocelyn lengthened and cooled down every muscle they'd used tonight to make sure no one suffered for the way she'd gotten lost in the music tonight. Dancing had always been her refuge, a way to forget the outside world. No matter how dark her thoughts were or how big her problems seemed, they all faded when she concentrated on placing her foot exactly so, or curving her back in the right form.

But that was her, and the last thing she wanted to do was have anyone hurt themselves because she'd been too lost in the music and memories to properly get them stretched after she'd worked them so hard.

Zoe's stare had turned into a smirk, and Jocelyn knew she was in trouble. So when everyone was done, towels put in the bags, shoes put on the feet, and saying their goodbyes at their cars, there was no way for her to avoid the final confrontation. Melodrama did not become her. Channeling her inner angsty thirteen-year-old wouldn't help the situation, so she let it go and figured she'd survived worse than a friend wanting details from a past that she hadn't thought about in years.

Still, from the gleam in Zoe's eye when they met in the parking lot, Jocelyn might be looking at something closer to the Spanish Inquisition.

"So do I have to call an emergency girl meeting, or are you going to tell me what in the world Dex was talking about when he came home and said he'd seen you at the diner with Sam and the two of you had been married in another lifetime?"

She could always count on Zoe to go straight for the gut.

"Yes, we were married." So that was how he'd manufactured a scenario that didn't spill his secret. Clever man. Sure, Dex had lied about how he'd found out, but at least it gave her the out she'd been looking for so she didn't ruin his surprise. She still wanted Zoe to enjoy her wedding surprise, even if it might cost Jocelyn her sanity in the process.

"And how is it that I've never heard about this

previous marriage?" Zoe planted her hands on her hips and stared at Jocelyn with narrowed eyes.

Jocelyn shrugged while looking around the emptying parking lot. Really, anywhere but at Zoe. "You never asked?"

"Come on!"

The indignation in her voice and the way she too sounded like a melodramatic thirteen-year-old made Jocelyn's gaze find her friend's face. Laughing was not going to help the situation, but Zoe looked like a little kid who was looking for the truth and was still being told that there definitely was a Santa. She couldn't help a small snicker.

That only made Zoe smack her in the shoulder.

"All right, look, let's go for a cup of coffee, and I promise I'll tell you all about it, what little there is. I don't talk about it because it was a long time ago and not one of my best life moments."

Zoe's face pulled into a frown. "I should tell you we don't have to talk about it if it hurts you, but I'm way too curious to be that nice."

Now Jocelyn really did laugh. "It doesn't hurt anymore. It's just not a really good memory. I'll meet you at the coffee shop, where we can discuss all the few details once I get a mocha frappe."

That seemed to at least get Zoe into her car and on her way to Jitters. Jocelyn took a moment longer than necessary to stow her gear into her back seat, then leaned against the car for another minute to contemplate how she was going to talk about the biggest mistake of her life.

Her phone rang in her pocket.

"Hello?"

"Don't you dare think about ducking out of coffee. I see you still standing at your car."

She sat down in the front seat. "I swear I'm coming. Stop creeping on me."

"Get your ass over here and I won't have to creep."

They hung up, and Jocelyn started her car. This would not be that hard. It would be good. She hadn't even told her mom what had happened, and she wouldn't be telling Zoe. All she had to do was satisfy the other woman's curiosity, and that could be done in a few sentences.

Zoe had already staked out a corner of the coffee house with the big comfy chairs. She had Jocelyn's coffee set up and had bought them each a marshmallow cereal treat. She meant business.

"I should hide things from you more often if it gets me the royal treatment." Jocelyn placed her purse at her feet on the floor and settled in for the short duration.

"Ha!" Zoe folded her legs under her and leaned back in the big ruby velvet chair like a queen on her throne. "If I find out you have other secrets, I'm just going to use interrogation tactics, not nice bribey kinds of things."

Jocelyn took a sip of her coffee and hummed her approval. This was perfect after the day she'd had.

"So spill." Zoe leaned forward with her own coffee in her hands and an expectant look on her open face. Her blonde hair was scraped back into a ponytail, and her face looked fresh despite the sweat Jocelyn had made her work up while cleansing her own demons. She would be a beautiful bride, and she was a great friend. If there was anyone Jocelyn could count on to be on her side, it was going to be Zoe, with her understanding nature and big heart.

Taking a long breath, Jocelyn held it for a moment, then let the words roll off her tongue in one long exhalation. "So, long ago, about eleven years ago, I was living in South Carolina and dancing while I went to college, and I met this guy while I was on the bar."

If possible, Zoe leaned even farther forward. She was going to fall off that chair any minute. "Wait. By 'on the bar,' do you mean you were serving drinks at a bar?" She tucked her hand under her chin. "I'm learning all kinds of stuff here."

Jocelyn rolled her eyes. "No, I was literally on the bar, like that movie *Coyote Ugly*. I worked in one of those places where the girls dancing on the bars are one of the draws to bring in the guys. So I danced on the bar."

"Shut the front door!" Zoe smacked her own knee, jostling her coffee in the process. She saved it at the last second, but Jocelyn had the feeling this conversation was going to last more than a few sentences if Zoe was going to question every word.

"You're killing me. I could have sworn I'd told you that before."

"Absolutely not. I would have remembered if you'd told me you were a bar dancer!"

"Fine, maybe I didn't tell you. But that's not the part you wanted to hear, right?"

"Right, right. It's not the big one, but I think I'm going to want to hear all about that later. For now, get on to the part where you were married and I had no idea."

Jocelyn blew out a breath. "So I'm dancing. It's a Friday night."

"Did you have to wear those little black shorts and the bustier? Was it that kind of place?"

"Lordy. Yes, I wore the shorts but the T-shirts were actually advertisements for the bar. It was in downtown Sumter, so it had to be enticing, but not a nudey bar. Jeez, it's not like I was stripping."

"That would have been awesome!" Zoe laughed loud at that, then stopped herself and kept just the grin on her face. "Right, sorry. Go on."

Jocelyn shook her head. "So I was dancing, and before you ask, it was eighties night, so we had on something close to what that girl in the old movie *Flashdance* wears, with the T-shirt hanging off her shoulder."

"I have the picture in my mind, and it's awesome. You should have come as that to the Halloween party."

"Good God."

"Kidding. Continue." She flapped a hand at Jocelyn as if she was being too slow in the storytelling.

"Fine. So I'm dancing, for the third time, and someone tried to grab my ankle. Hazard of the job, okay? And I started to fall, and this guy was standing to the side, and he literally plucked me out of the air and held me against him until I could get my breath."

Zoe fanned herself. "Oh, okay, now, that's pretty much swoon worthy. Tell me the guy was Sam."

The memory made Jocelyn smile for the first time since Sam had slammed into her a few hours ago. "It was Sam, not so built as now, but definitely built then. He and his buddies were on leave from Fort Sumter. They'd decided to hang out, and he witnessed the guy make the grab and managed to catch me before I hit the floor."

"That's kind of romantic, you know." A dreamy look crossed Zoe's face. The girl was a romantic through and through, no matter how much she had protested against it before hooking up with Dex. "I always knew Sam was attractive in a hard-worker kind of way, but thinking of him in the military and catching the girl from the bar is more romantic than I would have previously thought of him. He's always so serious."

"He was serious that night and about to take the guy out, but I had to stop him or I'd lose my job. I told him he could buy me a drink while I took a breather and got my bearings back."

Zoe's nose scrunched up. "And he bought that?"

"Yep, hook, line, and sinker."

With one eyebrow arched, Zoe smirked. "Either that or he was more interested in you than he was in fighting."

Jocelyn shrugged. "Either way, he started coming by as many nights as he was in town, and within a month we were dating and sleeping together. It didn't take much to convince me he was really good at anything he put his mind to."

"And he put his mind to you," Zoe said with a tone of satisfaction.

If only it had been that simple. "I guess." She needed to get off this subject or she'd flush at the memory of what exactly Sam could do if he put his mind to it. And he'd probably only gotten better as the years had gone on. God.

"Anyway, so we started seeing each other exclusively. From there it was a short jump to us getting married. His orders came in that he was shipping out. Since we were basically living together, he wanted me to get whatever benefits I could while he was out to sea. And this way we could stay in touch better because I'd be the wife, not just the girlfriend. I was giddy. He hadn't even met my mother yet, but I said yes without hesitating when he proposed to me over french fries at a local fast food restaurant."

"French fries? Seriously?"

"French fries." Jocelyn didn't even try to stop the smile blooming on her face at the memory of Sam popping a fry into her mouth. He'd followed it with a quick kiss and then asked her if she'd consider being his forever. She'd jumped into his lap, agreed between one salty kiss and the next, and then demanded a ring on her finger. They'd shopped that weekend at the mall and found something he could afford. It hadn't been expensive, but it was perfect. And she was going to make herself cry if she didn't move this story along.

"Mom was in that show in New York at the time, and I didn't want to disturb her. Or maybe that was my excuse for not telling her I had just jumped into marriage. But I loved him."

Zoe's smile softened. "He wouldn't be hard to love."

"Loved. Past tense. Anyway, so he goes on deployment, and six months turns into nine months. Things started getting bad between us, and when he came back we got a divorce. I haven't seen him since then and honestly would have thought he was still in the military. He was convinced at the time that he would be a lifer."

"I have a feeling you're leaving a lot out."

And she was—the lonely nights, not having friends

around, being a Navy wife with the other wives who had constant interaction with their husbands while she couldn't even get him to call her on her birthday. But that was all in the past.

"Not much. The divorce was amicable. It just wasn't working, and we didn't know each other well enough before he left. When he came home, it was better for us to part ways before we hated each other."

"It doesn't sound like he hates you now," Zoe pointed out. "Dex said he pretty much had stars in his eyes and was happier than he'd seen him in a long time. Not that he wasn't happy before, but there was something new in his eyes that's not usually there, and you know what a watcher Dex can be."

Yes, she knew Dex could be a watcher and that he also tried to make the people around him take themselves more seriously than they usually did. She was still on the periphery of the group at Decadence, sort of friends with Claudia and May, but definitely friends with Zoe. She was too busy to make much more of the relationships than that right now. But even that was more than she'd had before.

There was no point in thinking about "before."

"Yes, well, it won't stay, and I'm not getting involved again. Especially not with him."

Zoe just shot her a look over her coffee cup, but Jocelyn was not changing her mind. There were definite reasons why they weren't together anymore, and they hadn't changed in the ten years since she'd signed on the dotted line to end their marriage.

She changed the subject, and Zoe let her, thankfully.

Chapter Three

Class started in ten minutes. Sam had shown up at the studio early, hoping to catch a moment with Jocelyn, but she was more elusive than a sand rat. He stood in the front lobby smiling occasionally at one or another of the moms who clustered together in the chairs positioned to give a view of the small fry class. But they weren't looking at their munchkins. They kept glancing at him, smiling, then turning to whisper to each other. Maybe he should wait outside. But it was cold out there in the early December evening.

Finally, Dex showed up.

"Where have you been, man?" Sam asked impatiently, never so thankful for more testosterone in the air.

Dex glanced at his watch before giving him a sly smile. "It's only eight minutes until the class starts. I have plenty of time."

"Right," Sam said, checking his own watch. Had he really only been standing here for five minutes? It had felt like an eternity. "Yes, well, we shouldn't be late if we want to learn that dance for your wedding."

"Sure." Dex dragged the word out, and Sam had a feeling he had not heard the last of this.

Fortunately, he was saved by the other guys arriving. Logan and his brother Nate looked like they were having a good-natured argument, and Jack

27

followed along behind them, shaking his head. The wedding was set at Jack's inn on the outskirts of town, but he'd been dragooned into being one of the groomsmen, too. They were an eclectic group, but he considered these guys his friends.

"Would you look at the fancy man?" Nate said, circling Sam with his hands shoved into the pockets of his jeans.

Everyone took a moment to look, even the moms sitting in the chairs. Three or four whistles followed, but he couldn't be sure who they came from. Truthfully, he wasn't even sure he wanted to know.

"I was being grilled about not being on time and defending myself, so I didn't even notice." Dex gave Sam a once-over, too. It was all Sam could do not to go right back out to his car.

"What?" he said, not without a little belligerence in his voice.

"I just don't think any of us have ever seen you out of jeans and a T-shirt. The black pants go nicely with the light green button-down shirt. It's a perfect match for your eyes," Dex responded, and the men all snickered. "You even made sure the pants broke on the top of your spiffy black shoes. I'm impressed."

Sam scoffed at all of them. "I'm not dressed up. I'm not even wearing a tie. Besides, you dress fancier than this all the time."

Dex laughed. "I'm a lawyer. I have to be strangled by the tie. You, my friend, work in a metal shop. You'd get one of those things caught in a machine and be without a head."

Jack tapped Sam with the back of his hand to his arm. "Looking to impress a certain lady who runs around in that adorable see-through skirt?"

"You, too?" Sam asked.

"Just wondering. She is something to look at."

A growl rose in the back of his throat, but Sam was smart enough not to let it out. Instead, he turned as Flo came waltzing into the room, very ready to kiss her for interrupting the guys making fun of him.

"Oh, look at all these handsome men. And Sam, you look so debonair in your duds. Good choice on that shirt, darling. It matches your eyes perfectly and makes you look ready to take on the world." She beamed at them all, but he could swear he heard her mumble, "Or one stubborn girl," as they followed her down the hall to their practice room.

****

Why? Why must she be plagued by Sam in dress pants and that button-up shirt that only emphasized the breadth of his shoulders? He'd been well-built when they were twenty and he'd gone off to war in his fatigues, but now? He'd filled out. His shoulders were broader, his waist narrower, his face leaner, and his arms more muscular. The way he strode down the hallway made her think he was on a mission. It gave her just the slightest case of the shivers, though she very quickly blamed that on the near freezing temps outside. Yeah, that was it. Maybe she should check to see if the heater was working correctly.

At least she had sixth graders to look forward to. They were putting the finishing touches on their holiday performance. Entering the room marked "Plie," she nodded in approval as she made sure stretches were being done correctly and talking was kept to a minimum. While she wanted this to be fun, she also wanted the girls to take it seriously. Just then a rumble of laughter filtered through the soundproofed wall adjoining the room. Really? Was she going to have to go over there and tell them to keep it down?

Another rumble and the girls' heads all came up from the floor where they had been touching their noses to the ground in a straddle.

"I'll be right back," she said to all of them, straightened her spine, and exited the classroom. If Flo couldn't keep them in control, then they were going to have to practice when no one else was in the studio.

She was about to say just that when she caught sight of Sam whirling Flo around the floor, dipping her so her head almost touched the floor, then swinging her up to cradle her in his arms before swinging her legs behind his back.

It immediately threw her back to the day when she'd first seen Sam, in his dress whites, playing Dance Dance Revolution in an arcade. With his hands behind his back, he'd done each step as fluidly as a professional dancer and added little flourishes of his own as he'd hit every single mark, every single time. Her mouth had dropped open, and she had not yet gained control of herself when he turned around, those green eyes zeroing in on her and his smile almost blinding in the dim flashing lights of the game hall.

She shook her head to rid herself of that image. That was not now, and this was not the same thing. Why was he even here for dance lessons? There was nothing he didn't obviously still know how to do.

He'd told her once that his family had made him take ballroom dancing lessons, and she had almost swooned the first time he'd taken her into his arms.

They'd been at a club, and while other people were bumping and grinding, he'd led her in a salsa that had just about made her legs quiver, and not with exhaustion.

She shook that thought away, too.

"I'm trying to conduct a class next door," she said, directing her words at Flo but looking from one man to the next while she said them.

"We were just having a good time watching Sam show off his moves," Dex said, smoothly stepping in front of her with a smile and a hand on her shoulder.

She badly wanted to shake him off; however, she had to remember he was paying for these classes. He and his future wife might be her friends, but he was still a paying customer. Irritating him or his friends made no sense, especially when it wasn't him, or even the laughing, that had irritated her so much as having Sam in the building. And having him here shouldn't bother her at all. She no longer cared for him, no longer cared what he did or how he did it. Maybe she just needed to tell herself that a few thousand more times until she believed it.

"We'll be quieter," Dex continued, with that smile, but this time he slid his gaze to the right, in Sam's direction before making eye contact with her again and winking. Dammit.

"Thanks." Not the most brilliant of exits, but she had to go before she remembered anything else that Sam used to do or say. He'd left and had never come back, at least not to her.

****

He had expected razzing, and he got it. He expected ribbing and got that too. What he hadn't

31

expected was for Dex to pull him aside once everyone said goodbye at their cars.

"Can I have a minute?" Dex stood with his hand on the roof of his sporty car.

"Sure." Sam stuck his keys into his pocket.

"The girls have this thing they do called Emergency Girl Meetings, definitely with a capital letter for each word. I try hard not to ask too much about what they discuss, since most of it would probably make me blush, but I feel the need to offer you something like the name implies but with a more masculine tone." He chuffed out a laugh. "Guys' Beer Night, maybe?"

Sam chuckled. "I appreciate it, Dex, I really do. But there's no need. I think I have to face the fact that she won't even look at me. Things went to shit when we broke up, and she has every right to be pissed at me. Maybe I wouldn't have expected it this fierce all these years later, but maybe she's been fine until I came back and brought all those memories with me."

Dex tapped the roof of his car. "Look, if you don't want to do this dancing thing, I'm sure Flo could just write down the moves and you'd probably out-dance us all anyway."

Sam admitted, if only to himself, that the thought was tempting. But they were both grownups. He might have been a dick, but she was the one who had left him first. It shouldn't be that hard for them to be in the same zip code for the next few nights. "Nah. Though I appreciate the offer, it'll be fine. No need for beer night, either. Things didn't work before, and I'm sure they wouldn't have worked this time."

"You're giving up?" The tapping stopped abruptly.

"Just like that?"

He started to say yes, his brain thought it, his lips formed the beginning of the word, but then Jocelyn walked in front of the big glass window of the studio, backlit by the recessed lighting in the waiting room. Her translucent wraparound skirt swung at mid-thigh, her long muscular legs sleek in pink tights, her hair in a bun on top of her head. It all reminded him of when she'd taken classes at the local college. He'd come home from a long day in the field to find her using the short counter in the small kitchen of their apartment to do those squat things that put her rear end on the backs of her heels as she sank almost to the floor with her knees completely bent to make her shins almost parallel to the floor. She would pop up when he peeked over the top of the bar, and that smile would nearly blind him. No one's smile had blinded him since. Maybe he needed to be blinded again. And maybe, just maybe, she needed to do the blinding.

The thought made him stand taller. He was not a quitter. He had been once, and he was coming to realize that might have been the biggest mistake of his life. He wouldn't make it again without trying hard to avoid it. "No, as a matter of fact, I don't think I'm going to give up." He pounded a fist against his thigh. "In fact, I might just have to come up with a plan to not give up at all."

"Now, that's my boy." Dex slapped him on the shoulder eagerly. "Can I help? I was pretty successful myself at winning the girl, a few months ago."

"You're getting a little too close to that girly talking thing."

Dex laughed and mock-punched him in the

shoulder this time. "Never. I expect a full report tomorrow, though, and if I can help with anything at all, I'm game. After all you've done for our family, I could never pay you back fully, but this might be a down payment."

Sam thumped him back. "We'll see. In the meantime, you'd better get home before that girl you won starts wondering why you're home so late every single night the week before the wedding."

Dex got into his car while Sam remained outside looking into the studio, just watching the way his former wife flitted from one side of the waiting room to the other, righting magazines and lamps and chairs. Was it worth it to dredge up everything for a second chance that might never happen?

He'd like to think they were older now and therefore maybe better at talking. He'd made mistakes, yes, but he didn't think they were big enough to overshadow how he obviously still wanted her. Now it would just be a matter of finding out if her complete avoidance of him was because she didn't care at all, or because she still cared too much.

****

Another night. Another night of the guys dancing and the women standing at the window watching them with slight traces of drool on their chins. Lordy, this was not a meat market, though you couldn't tell that by the behavior of the participants lately. She'd even had one of the single moms approach her to see if any of the guys was single. As far as she knew, only Logan was definitely single. She shied away from wondering about Sam. Jack, Nate, and Dex were definitely taken. But she wasn't going to give that information out. The woman could go to one of those dating sites that were so popular these days.

Sam caught her in the hallway as he raced in from the parking lot.

"Sorry I'm late."

"I'm not the one you have to apologize to. Flo will be the one who's mad at you."

He flipped her a smile and wiggled his eyebrows at her. "I have a way with older women. I think I can handle her." He turned then to the group of senior high school students standing outside the room she was about to enter. "Ladies, don't let this one bully you. If I remember correctly, she has quite a set of lungs." And then he was gone.

She decided to ignore his idiocy even if, just for a second, she had wanted to smile. She did have a set of lungs and had used them often enough when they first moved in together. It wasn't her fault she had to bring him in time after time to put the toilet seat down after he was done. She didn't think that was exactly a story to share with the girls, so she shepherded them into the room with barres against the wall and floor-to-ceiling mirrors so they could watch themselves to make sure they had their moves right.

Slipping her feet into her jazz sneakers, she resolutely shut any and all men out of her mind. She had a performance coming up and a group of graduating seniors to put through their paces so they didn't fall off their pointe shoes.

She walked into a hushed room. All eyes were on her, wide and innocent-looking. "Are we ready to work? Are your stretches done?" she asked into the silence and was met with a few snickers behind young hands.

Mentally she rolled her eyes, even if she didn't do it physically. Lord save her from seventeen-year-old girls.

"Let's get a move on, or I'll have to use those lungs you all think are so funny."

Everyone stepped into position. She took them through the moves that would make up one of her most ambitious dances to date. She wanted to wow the people who attended the holiday show. This would definitely get the crowd to sit back in their seats. They had floor work, leaps, splits, and a few lifts to go with the pancake tutus and the pointe shoes. The girls were going to be magnificent, and she couldn't wait to see them shine. Only a little over two weeks left before the big show. If tonight was any indication, she was ready and so were they. She just had to get through this wedding, and then she'd be set.

****

Sam smiled as he entered the room, ready to charm Flo if necessary. It wasn't necessary, though, as she smiled at him and simply invited him to get into position. When Jack had been late yesterday, she'd shown that Jocelyn came by her lungs honestly. So why was he being given slack? Not that he was going to ask.

He stood near the other men, and they went through the nine moves they'd learned. There would be ten in all, from what he'd been told, basic moves done in sync sometimes and also individually. They were dancing to a popular wedding song, then kicking it up with a nineties boy-band song Zoe loved, ending with Jack and Sam standing on one side and Logan and Nate standing on the other side of a kneeling Dex in the middle of the floor with arms out, showboating. All in all, it wasn't difficult, but he thought Zoe would appreciate the effort.

When class was over, he grabbed his bag and sought out Jocelyn. He didn't see her in any of the glass-fronted classrooms. Catching Flo on her way out, he tapped her on the shoulder. "Any chance I could find out where Jocelyn is?"

"Depends." Maybe she didn't use the volume on him, but this time he did get a slight case of the frost.

"I just thought I'd say goodnight."

"Make sure you're nice about it." She eyed him up and down. "You might have forgotten what tomorrow is, but I don't think she ever has."

That brought him up short. Of course he knew what tomorrow was, but he was surprised to know Jocelyn's mother knew. He'd never even gotten a chance to meet her when they'd been married. He'd asked several times if Jocelyn wanted to drive up to meet Flo or have her fly down, but Jocelyn had always told him she wanted him to herself for a little bit longer. Thinking they had the rest of their lives together, he'd been sure there was plenty of time later to meet the in-laws. But that never happened, and now tomorrow would have been their anniversary, and Flo knew about it. Interesting.

"I will be nice. I promise."

"Keep this one," she said as she directed him toward a hallway and the door on the right, where the office was.

He popped his head around the doorway. He didn't say anything at first, just watched her working. The overhead light cast shadows on her cheekbones and on the hollow of her throat where he had loved kissing her. She'd make the most incredible little noises when he ran his hands over her shoulders or massaged her feet. They'd been something together, and maybe they could be again.

He rapped on the door frame. "Just wanted to say goodnight."

Her head snapped up. A glare narrowed her eyes. "Yes, goodnight."

"See you tomorrow?" he pressed.

"Probably not. I teach morning classes tomorrow. But Flo will be here in the evening."

"Okay." Should he mention the anniversary or not? The scowl had not yet left her face. Yeah, he didn't think he was going to mention it. Probably not a good idea. But the thought of it gave him an incredible idea.

****

Shutting down for the night, Jocelyn watched out of the corner of her eye as Sam stood in the parking lot looking for all the world like he was standing on the outside and wishing he could be invited in. Of course that was ridiculous. He'd always fit in everywhere and had a ton of friends, teammates, or just people in his life. She had been the one left alone. Besides, there was nothing for him here that he'd want.

She hated to leave him in the dark, but he'd just have to deal with the small carriage lights she'd installed at the entrance, once she turned out the front room lights.

She didn't wave, she didn't gesture to him at all, but he still lifted a hand as she turned out the last light. Walking into the back, she didn't look to see if he got into his car and left. It wasn't her business if he stood out there all night.

Her office beckoned with paperwork and counting up the receipts for the day, but she couldn't face it tonight. She promised herself she'd come in early tomorrow to get the business side of things out of the way before any dancers showed up.

A light in the storeroom flooded the back hallway. As she reached in to turn it off, she found Flo fluffing tutus.

"I wondered when you might come back this way." Flo turned with her hands on her hips. "Seeing the men out to their cars?"

"Of course not," Jocelyn said, wishing for something to do with her hands. She rolled her wrists, flexing and fisting her hands to relax the nerves in the tendons. "Just turning out all the lights and making sure everything is ready for tomorrow morning. I'll be coming in early to get paperwork done."

"Hmm."

Jocelyn ignored the noise, knowing that if she commented or tried to defend herself before she was even accused it would only make things worse. She was raw—raw from seeing him, raw from watching him dance, raw from listening to him laugh. Raw from watching him standing out in the parking lot like he was waiting for her to come out as she had when they'd first been married. They'd only had one car, so he'd pick her up from classes at the local college.

"I'll see you tomorrow," Jocelyn said, backing out of the room.

"Hold on."

Damn. She hadn't escaped fast enough.

"So he's the heartbreaker, isn't he?" Flo crossed

her arms over her chest.

Jocelyn did not want to have this conversation tonight. "Yes, but I don't want to talk about it."

"I never would have known if he hadn't said something to one of the other guys. I never saw a picture of him, never got to meet him."

"Yes, well, the ink was barely dry after our hasty seaside chapel wedding before he left on a ship, and then we'd fallen apart by the time he came back." The day she'd left the apartment with only the things she'd come with was the second hardest day of her life, but it had been necessary. And she'd never regretted the choice, just the events that had led up to it.

"You say that so matter-of-factly, like you weren't crushed when you came home."

"It was a long time ago, Mom."

Flo ran a hand down the side of Jocelyn's face, then caught a tear Jocelyn hadn't even realized had leaked out of the corner of her eye. "Maybe not so long ago."

Jocelyn swiped at her eyes. "Long enough. Now, please, let's just get this week over with so we can get back to the recital. I want the girls to shine. I might have bought a long-standing studio, but I'm going to have to show people I know how to pull off a recital, if they're going to stay. Can we concentrate on that, please?"

"If that's what you want," Flo said with her hand still on Jocelyn's. Sadness radiated from her voice, but Jocelyn could not do this tonight. Maybe not ever.

"It is."

"Okay, then." Flo fluffed two more tutus before turning back. "But you know I'm here if you need me.

I've always been here, even if you haven't always made use of me."

"I know." She hugged Flo, then left before the leaking could turn to honest-to-goodness crying. Her mom didn't know the half of it.

Chapter Four

After a restless night, Sam prayed that his automatic coffee maker had not decided that this morning was a perfect time to break. The smell of high-octane caffeine filtered through the house as he stumbled into the shower. The promise of coffee had him hustling through his morning routine. Throwing some eggs into a skillet, he scrambled, ignoring thoughts of Jocelyn and dancing and anything else that spoke of the past. He had jobs to do today and not a ton of time to get them done.

His assistant shop guy, Ethan, was leaving for his delayed combination honeymoon and family trip three weeks from now, and they had things to do before Sam was ready to take his own staycation over the Christmas break. He still didn't know what exactly he'd be doing during that week of vacation, but he'd think of something. Maybe something with Jocelyn…

He shouldn't think that far ahead if he couldn't even get her to look at him without those frown lines appearing between her eyebrows.

He was working on that but had no gauge for his amount of success.

Before he started for the day, though, he had an errand to run. Last night he'd gotten Flo's number from Dex. After some fast talking, he'd coerced her into meeting him at the studio at eight so he could deliver a package. She only agreed after telling him not to mess with her baby. He wasn't messing; he was trying to fix.

So before he got started on his own work in the shop behind his house, he sat in the parking lot behind the studio with a breakfast of tiny cinnamon muffins, a cup of dark roast vanilla coffee, and a small fruit salad in a champagne flute ready to hand over to Flo the minute she pulled up.

Her little speedster whipped into the parking lot. He was out of the car before she turned it off. Opening her door for her, he stepped back for her to exit.

"My, we're anxious, aren't we?"

"Yes. Absolutely." He wasn't trying to hide it, after all.

"She might hate me for this," Flo said with doubt coloring her voice.

"She won't. I brought her favorite foods and nothing else. I'm not trying to overwhelm her. I just want her to maybe think about if we made mistakes before that are worth talking out."

"Fancy words." She looked him up and down like she had the night before and made him feel two inches tall. "Do you mean them?"

He did not want to be in the parking lot when Jocelyn showed up; however, he knew he wasn't going to be able to leave without answering Flo's question. "Look, I was an asshole who thought he was doing the right thing, before. Obviously I did all the wrong things. I'd like to find out if there's a way we can patch things up, if not as a couple again, then at least as friends. I've never forgotten her, and just having her in my life would make me happier than should be allowed."

She squinted her eyes at him. "It's no wonder she

fell for you in such a short time."

He gave her his best smile, then ran back to his car for the small wicker basket that held Jocelyn's food, drink, and a small present. It was a small clay figurine she'd given to him on their only Valentine's Day together. Two otters held hands and floated on their backs together. He wasn't exactly happy to lose it, since it was one of the few memories she'd left him with, but if it was the beginning of some new memories, then it would all be worth it.

He set the basket down on her desk, kissed Flo on the check, and hustled out the door. When he was a block away, he watched in his rearview mirror as Jocelyn turned into her parking lot.

He hoped she'd be happy today.

The morning rushed by, with orders being pumped out of the CNC machine. Every couple of minutes he checked his phone, but there was nothing until after eleven, when she finally texted him to say—YOU DIDN'T HAVE TO. He wasn't sure what exactly that meant, but he did know that now he had her number, and she hadn't told him to go to hell. Two good things.

He'd been lucky to get Ethan back working for him. The guy knew what he was doing and was more than proficient at his job, plus he was a quick learner. Sam had hesitated at the beginning, not sure if he could trust someone so young, but he was glad he'd taken a chance and that the kid had come back for his little family—the little family he watched round the corner of the house with a basket. Almost every day Delly brought Ethan's daughter to the backyard, where Sam had installed a picnic table in a screened-in gazebo so lunch could be this kind of family affair. It had been a rough several months for the three of them, but it looked like things were working out now. Their daughter, Phoebe, was adorable and deserved both parents, no matter how young they were.

He flipped a wave to Delly, and she waved back. Turning to Ethan, he signaled him to shut off the machine and remove his ear and eye protection.

"They're here," he said once his apprentice stepped away from the machine.

"Thanks. Is it okay if I still take a lunch today, even though it's my last day for a little while?"

"Yeah, kid, go on out."

Delly peeked her head around the edge of one of the double barn doors that fronted the shop. "Sam, I brought enough for you, too."

"Nah, I've got work."

"And you have to eat," she said. Not for the first time he acknowledged her stubborn streak. It would serve her well if she and Ethan were to make it in their brand-new marriage.

He was about to say no when Phoebe reached out her arms to him and fell forward. He caught her at the last second.

The cheeky smile and the chubby arms were his undoing as she hugged him and gave him a smacking kiss on the cheek.

"Okay, I can take a small break. And with Ethan here working his ass off, we're farther ahead of schedule than I had anticipated."

Delly hugged Ethan and then rested her head on his shoulder, looking up at him with adoring eyes. Long ago, Jocelyn had looked at him like that. He hoped that, since these two had gone through their biggest trouble earlier, they'd realize they could get through anything. He wasn't even sure what he and Jocelyn hadn't survived, but he knew his own part of it. To this day he wondered what would have happened if he'd trusted more and worried less.

Thankfully Delly interrupted his thoughts. Unfortunately, her topic wasn't that far off from what he'd been pondering.

"Dex mentioned that your ex-wife lives in town. I didn't know you used to be married." She dished out potato salad and laid out sandwiches as Ethan cranked up the space heater in the corner. When the weather turned cold, Sam had bought collapsible windows to install inside the screens so that they could still use the building without feeling like they were intruding on his house. That seemed to be important to Ethan. It hadn't cost much to accommodate him.

"Yeah, she owns that studio where Zoe does her booty-shaking stuff."

"Booty-shaking stuff?" Delly asked, then laughed as she set root beer bottles in front of everyone. Phoebe sat on her lap with a sippy cup in her hands, banging it on the wooden table.

Ethan placed a hand on the cup and said, "No," softly. The little girl looked up at him, smiled, and popped the thing into her mouth.

Ethan had grown up a lot since he'd started here, and Sam liked seeing the changes. Now if he could just get them onto a different topic. He didn't want to talk about Jocelyn.

It wasn't to be, though.

"Why are you guys divorced?" Delly asked, feeding a small piece of cheese to the child and taking a bite of her tuna fish sandwich.

"Delly," Ethan said, a clear warning in his tone.

"It's okay," Sam said. Was it, though? Sam wondered even as he murmured the words. This could have been him and Jocelyn ten years ago, minus the kid. He hadn't even thought that until he'd seen her two nights ago. His whole perspective and thought pattern seemed to have changed, now that he knew she was within reach.

"I went off to war shortly after we got married. We'd only known each other for about a month. It was a quickie wedding, but I was sure she'd be there when I got back. But then guys started getting those Dear John letters from their girls back home saying they'd found new guys or wanted to date other people because they were lonely. I didn't want to hear it, so I didn't write, and she didn't write me, either. I can't say I was surprised when I came home to an empty apartment and divorce papers. I signed them because I was an asshole who hadn't had any faith in her. I never sought her out again. I assumed she'd gone off to do her own thing, and I lost the chance to be a part of whatever that was." There was more than that, but it was what he was willing to share. The rest really made him sound like a jerk who had thought he had to protect a strong woman from everything, like a neanderthal.

"Well, that sucks." Ethan took a pull on his root beer.

"Yeah, I was an idiot."

"But you never looked for her? Did she ever say why exactly she left?"

"Maybe she found another guy and didn't want to have to tell me we'd made a mistake, not when I was trying to stay alive."

"I'd want to know," Delly said, pulling a jar of pickles from the cooler and handing them to Ethan to open.

"I'd want to know, too." Ethan smiled. "I'd want to know enough to see if she still had feelings for me. I mean, I heard she avoids all eye contact with you and barely talks to you. There's got to be more there than nothing if she won't look at you, man. I bet she'd talk to you if you tried to talk to her. What do you have to lose?"

Like he needed dating advice from some young pup. But then he realized maybe Ethan was speaking from experience. He'd never tried to find out about where Delly went when she left him, and then he was hit with a baby without a clue. Not that Sam thought they'd had a baby. He certainly hoped Jocelyn would have told him if they had a child. He would not be happy to be a part of one of those secret-baby romance things his sister devoured.

"I guess I don't have anything to lose, especially since I won't see her again after this week. I have a feeling her doors would already be closed to me if I hadn't paid in advance for the class and wasn't a friend of Dex's."

His phone pinged with a text. CAN YOU COME BY?

Same number as before. Either she wanted to smack him or maybe they'd actually talk, but he wasn't missing this. He texted back for the time and she said, ASAP. He jumped up from the table. "Thanks for lunch and the conversation, guys, but I just got an invite to come to the studio. I'll be back a little later, if you don't mind continuing on with the Jameson order."

Delly waved him away. "I'm sure Ethan will be fine, and we're going back home. Go see what she wants."

Hopefully it was him…

****

Pacing was not going to make this nervous energy go away. Jocelyn told herself the same thing for the seventh time, but it still was not making a difference. She finally took herself into the smallest of dance rooms and did a dance from one of her college classes that left her sweating but feeling much better. She grabbed her towel off the barre to her left just as she spotted Sam walking through the front door.

They stared at each other through the glass pane separating them, and Jocelyn honestly did not know what to think or do. When she'd arrived to the same breakfast they'd had on the first day of their honeymoon and the figurine with the otters holding hands, she sniffled a few times but kept her eyes dry. But when she opened the card he'd left along with them, it was like freaking Niagara Falls. He'd signed it "Isle Of View," a phrase they'd often said to each other instead of "I love you" because they'd liked to joke with each other that way. They'd even had a little snow globe with a small island complete with two sunbathers and a palm tree on it that they would hide from each other in places, just to see the other one smile when they found it.

Why had that all fallen apart as soon as he flew away from her?

She had to know, and that was why she'd invited him down here. That's why they were staring at each other across the room now.

He pulled open the glass door to the room and stepped in. "I hope you liked the breakfast."

"I did. Thanks." And now she felt horribly awkward, because today would have been their anniversary, but it wasn't anymore because they were divorced. She hadn't gotten him anything, thinking he wouldn't remember and knowing that it didn't matter even if he did. They were no longer married.

"What about the card?" He walked toward her on those long, strong, lean legs, the ones she'd wrapped herself around countless times as he rode her hard, just the way she liked it. With his long fingers trailing along the barres attached to the walls, she never thought she would be jealous of an inanimate object, but there you had it. She was. Desperately.

Heat grew in her stomach, and she couldn't find it in herself to say no when he moved across the room instead of around it and came to stand in front of her.

His palm cupped her cheek, his fingers smoothing back a few stray hairs that always seemed to escape her severe bun. He brought his other hand up, smoothing his palm down her neck, dragging sensations riotously through her system as he settled his long fingers at the base of her skull, just under her bun. It was one of the most sensitive areas on her body, and he'd remembered. His face hovered inches above her, his cheeks, eyes, lips filling her vision as he came closer and closer until all she could do was close her eyes and hold on as he laid his lips on hers.

Flashes went off behind her closed lids, tiny sparks of light that made her dizzy and left her craving far more than just a kiss. Wrapping her arms around his waist, she leaned into him. His answering groan rumbled her chest. She wanted to crawl inside him.

The taste of him was the same, and she knew it instantly. After years of eating and drinking, and even kissing a few other men, she shouldn't be able to remember with absolute clarity the taste of his mouth, but there was no denying that she did.

His hand moved from her neck to her back, then smoothed down to the edge of her ballet skirt. She couldn't let him go any farther, but God she wanted to.

"Meet me tonight," he murmured against her lips. "Meet me tonight, and we'll see if we remember the rest of each other."

She shoved him away from her, outrage coursing through her. "Really, you waltz back in here after ten years and expect me to fall into bed with you just because you regifted me something I gave you years ago that you should have thrown away and you remembered what we had for breakfast? I'm not that easy." She straightened her skirt, lifted a hand to her hair, and realized that the pins had been removed. She'd find them later. Fortunately, she had others in her desk. Glancing at the clock, she took another step back. "I have class in ten minutes. I suggest you take your leave before the preschool moms start asking if you're single. I'd have to tell them yes, and if your phone number just happens to end up in some of their phones, it won't be my fault."

She looked away from the hurt crossing his face. She had to protect herself. She had to. If he didn't get that, then it wasn't her fault. She'd given herself fully to him, and he'd thrown her away to go play soldier, forgetting that he had a wife at home waiting anxiously to hear just one word from him. A letter, a phone call, something. But she'd gotten nothing, and now he'd get nothing.

He didn't move for long moments, but then she heard the glass door open. She forced herself to continue looking at the computer screen in front of her, to concentrate on queuing up the right music instead of trying to get just one more glimpse of him in the mirrored wall as he walked away.

****

Well, that had all gone to shit. Sam hit his steering wheel hard enough to bruise the side of his hand. What the hell had he thought she was going to do? Just fall right into his arms because he remembered their anniversary after ignoring her when they were actually married? He was an idiot.

He should have stuck to his original plan. He'd planned to walk in, start a conversation with her, and see if they still had anything to work with or if he was the only one who still felt anything. His thought was to feel her out, not feel her up, and instead he was back at square one minus seven. Christ, she might not even let him back in the studio after that.

At least she wasn't working tonight…

****

Jocelyn would gladly give her best pair of pointe shoes to not have to be at the studio tonight. But Flo had come down with a cold and was achy, not exactly the best shape in which to teach. Unfortunately, that left Jocelyn teaching the men while she had one of the seniors fill in for her on her seventh grade class.

She checked the notes one more time with Noelle, making sure she understood the turn on the second eight-count.

"I've got this, Miss Jocelyn. I promise. And the girls know this dance by heart. I'm probably just going to be correcting here and there, not teaching them anything. The show's only two weeks from Saturday. I danced with you for years and know you wouldn't let them come this far without having a grip on the steps well enough to do them in their sleep." The girl smiled at her, and Jocelyn tried to smile back.

She had worked here for eight years before she bought the studio from Beulah. They knew her style and the way she taught. She shouldn't be concerned with turning her girls over to the girl who had danced here since she was three. And she wasn't, she was just concerned with teaching the guys. Or rather, one guy in particular.

As if she'd conjured him up, Sam strode through the front doors. She felt him before she saw him. He'd always had a presence she was drawn to. They could be in separate rooms in their small apartment or in opposite ends of a friend's house and she just knew where he was. She'd thought leaving him would break that connection, but apparently it was still as strong as ever.

****

Jocelyn glanced his way before bending her head back to the girl standing next to her and talking about some dance moves. He wanted to say hi to her, see if they could at least find some friendly ground to start from, but she shut him out and down with one turn of her back.

He was being stupid if he thought talking to her about what really happened to their marriage would make a difference. No, they had never talked about it. She hadn't even left him a Dear John letter at all. She'd simply been gone, the only reminder of her the scent of her perfume in the air and a set of papers set squarely on the dining room table where he'd kissed her neck, stroked her thighs, and made love to her on more than one occasion. He still had that dining set. It was in his game room now, crowded with schematics for parts and pieces he made out in the shop, but he still had it.

Logan entered the building and slapped him on the back. "Ready for another night of showing us all up?" his friend asked. "I had no idea you had those kinds of moves."

Jocelyn half turned her head his way, then jerked her attention back to the papers in front of her.

"Yeah, well, it's been a long time since I danced, but it came back to me pretty quickly. You're no slouch yourself out on the floor, for a builder guy."

Logan laughed. "Yeah, maybe that will get the ladies to notice me, since working in tight T-shirts while I lay bricks hasn't exactly had them flocking to my door."

Sam laughed with him. "Maybe you should try it without the shirt; I heard that's what got Claudia to notice your brother Nate."

The man in question strolled in with Jack. "Claudia noticed me way before that moment at the stop sign. She just wouldn't admit it. And if Logan would step up, he could get the girl he's been eyeing for a few months, too."

The tops of Logan's cheeks flushed red as he stole a quick glance at Jack, then looked away. Sam didn't know anything about this mysterious woman, but if she was connected to Jack, then it had to either be his sister, who'd had a child a few months ago, or it was Adele, his right-hand woman at the inn. Either would be an interesting match for the man who seemed to keep mostly to himself.

Dex came in, and their party was complete. Jocelyn finally turned to them with a smile that bypassed him. She met each of their gazes while flitting right over his. Fine, it really had been a bad idea to think about trying to talk to her. Things had worked out for Delly and Ethan, but they'd been together longer than he and Jocelyn and not apart as long. Their water under the bridge was a small puddle compared to the flood of his ruined marriage.

He kept to the back of the line as all the guys followed Jocelyn into the studio. Dress shoes came out and were put on as Jocelyn headed to the front of the room to stand before the wall-to-wall mirror.

"I laid down the floating floor so your shoes don't scratch up mine. Let's do some stretches, and then we'll get started. Flo isn't feeling well tonight, so I'm taking over the class. I have the dance on a clipboard, so we should be able to make some progress and at least go over the steps you've already learned."

The night had just gotten infinitely more interesting and more difficult all in one moment.

Chapter Five

Within moments of class starting she understood why Flo was keeping the dance to ten moves and varying them only a little. Dex was good, Logan was better, Sam the best, but Jack and Nate hopefully had talents in other areas. She couldn't fault any of their enthusiasm, though, and she'd be able to give the two a few pointers to make up for their lack of rhythm on the dance floor.

She hoped they were better in bed than on the dance floor. The thought made her blush, and her glance shot to Sam without a second's hesitation. He had rhythm both on and off the dance floor. Rhythm that had made her writhe in ecstasy every time they'd been together, from the very first time.

He caught her looking at him and grinned as he executed a complicated grapevine with side slide. It was a move they'd done at the small party they'd had at the officer's club after getting married. People had cat-called and hooted and howled as they had swooped and swirled around the floor in a dance they'd never practiced. But they'd been so in tune with each other they didn't need to do anything but have him lead and her follow.

She'd never found anyone like him again. That was a good thing, she told herself as she worked hard to not scowl at him.

"Okay, let's try the next step." They started with the arms. After watching Jack and Nate get it wrong, she gave them a different set of hand movements and made a note on Flo's chart. It would look good.

"Start at the beginning and throw that on the end."

She sent them through the paces three more times before she was satisfied they were getting it. With only three nights left, they'd have to step it up if they wanted to get it all down. She cut the next four steps and had them repeat what they'd just done. It worked with the beat and also gave some of them more confidence, since it wouldn't be doing new combinations but just remembering to repeat.

She got them into cool-down mode, sent them through the paces to loosen up the muscles they'd used, then thanked them and dismissed them.

She'd survived the class.

She hoped she was alone when she turned again but wasn't entirely surprised to find Sam across the room, leaning on the doorway with his arms and ankles crossed. His presence had lingered.

"We don't get stickers like those cute kindergarteners you were teaching the other night?" he asked, his voice light and teasing.

"Nope. Stickers stop at third grade, and stamps start." Maybe if she kept the conversation light he would leave sooner. They had three more nights, and then he'd be gone. She was aware he was in the area, but he'd been in the area for four years now, from what Zoe had told her, and they'd never crossed paths before. They didn't have to start now, if she had any say.

"So what comes after stamps? I can't imagine a seventeen-year-old wanting her hand stamped for doing a good job."

"They don't get anything but the satisfaction of a job well done, and sore muscles."

"That doesn't seem very fair. They should get something. What about a shout-out on social media?"

She scoffed but then couldn't help laughing. Ashley, her texting queen, would love to have Jocelyn hash tag her on the Internet for doing a good job. She was looking at professional dancing colleges, and it probably wouldn't be a bad thing for her to have people talking about her and her talent for the school to see.

"I missed that sound when I came home to the empty apartment. It was the first thing I wanted to hear when I didn't see you at the drop-off point, when we flew into the airport and everyone else had someone waiting for them. I thought maybe you just had something to do or maybe hadn't heard we were coming home a few days early. I was going to come into the apartment and surprise a laugh out of you, just to hear it for the first time in months."

Every muscle in her back went rigid. "Yes, well, it didn't happen that way." She busied herself cleaning up the paperwork on the clipboard, straightening the pencils on the desk, moving the mouse around on its ballet mousepad.

"No, it didn't." She felt him walk farther into the room. His voice was closer when he said, "I never asked why. I was willing to let it all go, but now that I've seen you again, I don't think I can do that anymore. I want to ask now why you left without a word to me. If I ask, will you answer?"

Her stomach rolled, her hands grew clammy, and her ears rang, but she turned to face him. "No, I don't think I will answer, so you might as well not ask."

"That simple, huh? You tell me to back off, and I do it because that's what you expect?" He uncrossed his arms and came farther into the room.

"That's how it worked before. I don't see why we have to change tactics now. I didn't ask why you never wrote or called me on my birthday when I repeatedly heard all the other wives and girlfriends being in constant contact with their significant others. I wasn't significant enough for you to even write a letter, so I don't think you have the right to ask anything." She turned to the computer in the corner to shut it down for the night, expecting him to leave. "I don't think we have anything more to talk about, and I have to close. Hopefully Flo will be back tomorrow, and she can teach everyone the rest of the dance. Have a good night."

She walked away, horrified that she had said so much. Once she'd started she hadn't been able to stop. Not that it would change anything. But she'd just exposed herself for absolutely nothing.

****

For one agonizing breath, Sam thought his heart might have stopped. Had she really thought that? God! He was in motion before he could stop himself. Grabbing her upper arm, he turned her to him.

She yanked her arm out of his grasp. "Don't you dare! You lost all rights to touch me."

He lifted his hands. "Sorry. I'm sorry." He ran his hand over the back of his head. "You just took me off guard, and I can't let you continue to think you meant nothing to me." He backed up with his hands in the air. "You meant the world to me, Jocelyn." He put his hand out when she scoffed. "I'm not making that up. I am completely serious. You were my everything. Every day started with me marking a calendar to count down the days until I could see you again. I didn't want you to be touched by the ugliness over there. And a lot of those men writing and calling their wives were messing around on them with any girl who would spread her legs."

"And you didn't participate at all?" she asked skeptically.

She hadn't walked away, so he considered that a small victory. "No, I didn't. I wanted you with every breath of dirt and dust I took. I wanted the smell of you, your smile, your touch. Instead I got grime and death and nothing good. I was coming home to you to get out of the military. I wanted to start a life with you to erase all that—and I came home to nothing."

"And how the hell was I supposed to know that, Sam?" she demanded.

It was the first time she'd said his name, and it sang through his blood.

She continued before he could say anything. "I sat at home for almost nine months, waiting for anything from you. The smell of you on a letter, a smile in a picture, a touch through the phone. And you gave me nothing." One tear escaped from her glassy eyes which she angrily wiped away. She stalked to the front door and shoved him out in front of her. "Nothing. And you want to talk about being left with nothing? Try being pregnant and not knowing how to get in touch with your husband with the happy news, or with the horrible, gut-wrenching news that you lost that one part of him you thought you'd at least get to carry with you." She slammed the door in his face.

He'd thought taking a breath was agonizing before, but it was nothing compared to the jagged knives cutting through his lungs at this very moment when he realized he'd lost so much more than he had ever known.

****

"Stupid, stupid, stupid! I can't believe I did that!" Jocelyn wanted to kick something but couldn't afford to hurt her toes. And there was nothing in the studio she was willing to throw. She'd stormed into the back of the building to get away from Sam. She was not leaving out the back door until she heard his truck pull away. She would not see him again tonight. She swore to herself that tomorrow she would avoid him or at least act like nothing had happened. Knowing him as she did, he would most likely not go with her plan, but she didn't care, at this point. No one knew she'd been pregnant, not even her mother. She had wanted to tell Sam first, and since he never called, she had tried to get hold of him through the main office. They had sent a message out to the field, but she'd never heard anything back. She didn't have the address. She'd finally worked up the courage to admit to the perfect military wives around her that her husband hadn't sent her a single letter, to ask for the address, when she started bleeding like someone had stabbed her.

She'd cried and cried between praying. And then she'd taken herself to the hospital, so yes, other people knew she'd been pregnant, those at the hospital, but no one who cared about her as a person. They'd asked if there was anyone they could call for her, and she refused to answer.

She'd gone back to the empty apartment, packed

up her things, called a lawyer to start the proceedings, and then hidden at a beach cabin for three weeks until she could get herself together.

In the end, she realized it was better that she had lost the baby. Staying just for the sake of the child in a marriage that was doomed to fail would have made no one the winner.

A knock sounded on the back door behind her. She jumped, ready to bolt to the front if Sam thought she had any desire to finish this conversation. She would just hide out until he went away. She'd hide for the next few days, too. The only time she would have to interact with him would be at the wedding, and even then there would be more than enough people around her that she could keep him away from her.

It was a solid plan and made her feel better. Until her phone rang.

Taking it off the desk, she saw it was Zoe calling. She hadn't missed coffee, had she?

"Hello?" She really hoped that her voice didn't reflect the tears she still had not allowed to fall.

"I'm at the back. You're either going to open the door or I'm going to get the spare key from your mom."

Jocelyn forced words out through her quivering lips. "I have too much to do tonight, and then I'm going home to sleep. It's been a long day, with taking that class tonight. I just need some sleep."

"That is totally lame, and you know it. The Kissinger grapevine works a hell of a lot faster than you think, especially when Sam's first call was to me, thinking that you might need a friend right now."

Damn him. "I'm fine. I don't know why he thinks I need a friend. He tried to talk to me about why I divorced him. I told him he had no right to answers, and then I pushed him out the door."

"We're approaching that info I told you that you were holding back from me when we had coffee the other night. I don't want to set you off, so I'm just going to say that you need to open the door, and you need to open it now. Or I will so totally go to your mom."

What did Sam tell her? Did it matter? She still had to open the door or risk her mother coming in with Zoe to find out what was going on with her. As far as anybody else knew, she and Sam had just not made it. She didn't want anyone to know any more than that. She hadn't even wanted Sam to know, but she'd blown that one right out of the water.

"I'll unlock the door, but I reserve the right to remain silent if I don't want to answer any question you pose."

There was a beat of silence. "I'm waiting."

Jocelyn approached the back door, half afraid Zoe would have Sam trailing in behind her. Her friend fancied herself a matchmaker after she'd finally got Nate and Claudia to notice what they'd had for years. And she might not have been instrumental in Chelsea and Jack realizing they loved each other, but she'd had a hand in helping them along, nonetheless.

This was not the same at all, though. There was nothing left to salvage. There would be no returns, no exchanges of words, no recommitments, no long-lost love come home. And she was fine with that.

Or at least that was what she told herself until she opened the door and saw not only Zoe but also Chelsea, Claudia, and May.

She was not going to get out of this without crying, so she might as well hydrate herself while she had the chance.

"Come on in. I only have water, no coffee, sorry." She left the door open, figuring they would follow her in.

Zoe handed her a latte fixed just the way she liked. "We stopped before we came over."

"You didn't have to do that. You didn't even have to get everyone out of their homes to come here. I'm fine." Or she would be as soon as she sold the studio, packed up her stuff, and went to bury her head in the sand somewhere very, very far away. The way her life worked, she would never be able to go into a store around Kissinger again without seeing Sam. He'd be everywhere, even if she'd never seen him around before now. It was how things happened in her life, and she wouldn't be able to face him after the way she had just acted.

What if Flo found out? She'd never forgive her for keeping something like that to herself when she could have helped her through the sadness.

She led them all through the front waiting room and unrolled the shades she used during the day if the sun shone in too brightly. They didn't have complete privacy, but it was better than feeling like she was on display for the whole town to see, like living inside a fishbowl.

"Do you want to tell us what happened, hon?" Claudia said as she seated herself in a chair to Jocelyn's left. Zoe sat at her feet with her head on Jocelyn's knee. May took the chair on her right, and Chelsea sat on the arm of Jocelyn's chair and ran a hand up and down

Jocelyn's arm.

She'd never been so surrounded. When she was younger, she'd had a ton of dance friends, but the studios where she'd danced had so much competition that no one ever really told anyone their secrets. It was all surface niceness and spoken good lucks while hoping that a step went wrong or a foot was misplaced so the lead didn't go to someone else.

When she'd been a military wife, there were plenty of women who were friends with each other and had been friends as they moved from base to base, like cliques. Most of them were officers' wives, though, and she'd been so young and unsure of herself.

But here, here was friendship and love and acceptance in a way she had not let herself believe she was a part of. She'd held herself at arm's length, except for going to coffee with Zoe, and even then she'd only told her things that were safe. So could she change a lifetime of keeping to herself and finally open up, or would she keep herself in her rut and never get the most of life she could?

With that thought, she broke and told the whole sobbing story.

****

"Man, I was hoping we'd find you here. It's the last bar in town, and I wasn't sure where else to look." Logan slid onto a stool to the right of Sam, while Dex sat on his left.

Sam stared straight ahead, not wanting to talk to anyone for a good long while.

"A beer for me, a whisky for the guy in the tie, and another of whatever this one is having," Logan called to the bartender.

The guy nodded and went to go pour. Sam sat in silence, and the two men at his sides followed suit. Their drinks came, and still they didn't say anything. Sam threw a few bills on the bar, then rose to leave. Dex's hand clamped on his forearm.

"Not yet. You're not driving home like this, to sit in an empty house."

Sam shook him off. "I didn't ask for you two to come find me. I have things to think about. I'd do better thinking about them on my own."

"Yeah, well, the womenfolk got a call, and then Dex and I got sent out to find you because we're the only two without kids to look after. Lucky us, huh?" Logan picked at the label on his beer.

Sam choked back the moan that had almost escaped him. My God, if Jocelyn had been able to have their child, he or she would have been as old as Claudia and Nate's boy. He pinched the bridge of his nose. He couldn't think that way.

"I think I'm going to have to just show up for the wedding and do the dance from what I remember, Dex. Sorry. I can't go back to the studio."

"What happened?" Dex asked. "Zoe only told me that you called her to tell her Jocelyn needed a friend. You guys didn't fight, did you?"

If only it had been that easy. "No, but I don't think she's going to want to ever see me again. It would be better if I tried to give her what she wants now, since I didn't when we were married."

"Cryptic is not exactly like you. It couldn't have been that bad."

"Oh, it was that bad. It's not enough that I didn't call her on her birthday, or that I never wrote to her, and left her alone in a place where she knew no one."

"But that was your job. You didn't know you'd be deployed right then." Logan took a gulp of beer.

"No, I didn't, but I thought I was protecting her from all the shit that was happening during the war. Instead I was just pushing her farther and farther away." He couldn't talk about the lost baby. It wasn't his story to tell. "Needless to say, she needed me and I bailed."

"But she was the one who walked away, right?" Logan asked.

"Logan, I think it might be more complicated than that. Why don't we see Sam home, and hopefully things will look better in the morning."

"I doubt it." Sam rose from his stool and patted both men on the back. "I appreciate the offer to get me home, but I walked to clear my head. I'll walk back to do the same thing."

He exited the bar, turning toward home. Where no one and nothing was waiting for him. That wasn't entirely true. He had a thriving business, a nice home, good friends, and had made a good life for himself. Now that he knew what he'd turned his back on, he'd have to give himself some time to grieve those lost opportunities, then get back to his world. After the wedding.

Chapter Six

"Will Sam be here tonight?" Jocelyn heard Flo ask as the door closed on the last night of instruction for the wedding dance.

She didn't need to hear the answer to know it would be no. There was no way Sam would come back after the way she had sent him off two days ago. Last night he'd begged off for an abundance of work, without raising too many eyebrows, but tonight she'd heard nothing. What was he doing instead?

Talking with the girls had helped a lot and had unburdened her of the continued sorrow she had carried around for years without knowing it. She'd never talked about the miscarriage with anyone but professionals, and so to have feminine hands stroking her hair and her arms while she cried over the loss alleviated so much that she hadn't even been aware she was carrying.

The sorrow didn't leave her entirely. She would still look at Claudia's son every once in a while and think that if she'd had the baby it would be Justin's age. But it didn't hurt as much now.

It wasn't a secret festering like a splinter. She felt almost cleansed to have shared it.

Did Sam have someone he was able to talk with about it? She shouldn't even worry about that, after his crappy excuses for why he didn't contact her in the months he was away even though they were married, but it still poked at her brain. Since he hadn't told Zoe why Jocelyn needed a friend, she assumed that in this instance he was still the same as he'd been when he was younger. He fully believed that each person had their own story, and while he'd listen endlessly, he never shared anything that was told to him in confidence. She had a feeling he would not tell a single person and would instead bottle it up to deal with it alone, as he did with many other things.

She wanted to not care about that, but she just couldn't bring herself to be that cold. There had been a time that he was her whole world, and seeing him hurting, especially if she'd done it, was not something she could live with. This was not about getting even, or at least it shouldn't have been. She had to fix it.

"I'm heading out," she said to Flo when she peeked her head into the room where they were finalizing the steps. "I don't have any more classes tonight, and I have something I have to do."

"Bye, sweetie. I'll lock up," Flo called back before returning to her guys, who were looking better than even last night. Maybe she really should consider offering some ballroom dancing classes in the evenings. It would be a great couples' class, and she could get it up and running just in time for men to give to their wives as a Valentine's Day present.

She'd have to think about it. But for now she had a destination in mind, and she had to get there without chickening out.

She got the address from Zoe, who nearly screamed her ear off. Jocelyn tried to explain that she was only going over to apologize, but she ended up hanging up on her friend because there was no getting through to her.

His house was about fifteen minutes away—two towns and fifteen minutes. That was the way of Central Pennsylvania.

The house was dark when she pulled up to the curb. And there she did almost chicken out. But a light spilled from the big barn in the back. Most likely he was working. If she didn't do this now, she wasn't ever going to do it. She acknowledged that if she backed out, a little part of her would die for him. This did not mean they were getting together, only that she cared enough about him to not leave him hurting for years like she had.

Walking up the driveway and then around the house, she skirted a gazebo in the backyard with a picnic table and a small heater inside. Her sneakers made no sound on the pavement as she walked along the edge of the grass and followed the golden spill of light falling from the large windows on either side of the double barn doors.

Drawing in a deep breath, she braced herself as she knocked on one of the doors. Nothing happened. A low whirring noise reached her ears. She knew nothing about what Sam did as a business, so she couldn't identify what she was hearing. She tried again, banging on the doors this time.

And then he was standing there in low-slung jeans, a long sleeved T-shirt, and work boots. He had safety glasses on, and his hair stood up on end. Earplugs on a bright orange string rounded out the Working Man's Outfit. If she were being honest, she'd have to admit she wasn't sure she'd ever seen anything more appealing in all her life.

She mentally shook her head at herself. She was not here to admire him, or his attire, or the way his muscles bunched and flexed when he folded his arms over his chest and widened his stance like he was waiting for her to land another blow.

"Mind if I come in for a minute?" She clasped her own arms across her chest. Either the temperature had just dropped significantly or she was being attacked by a case of the nerves. She was pretty sure it was the nerves.

He backed up enough to let her through the door, then closed it behind her. Turning away from her, he took out his earplugs and removed the safety goggles. When he faced her again, he had a ridge line on his nose, but that was not something she was going to say even if it would potentially break the ice and the deafening silence.

"I like your shop." She looked from left to right in a sweeping arc, not looking at him but taking in the huge machines, the shine and the obvious care he gave the things that belonged to him. She'd been in shops before, professional ones, when she went to tour shoe manufacturers, and none had ever been this clean or this organized.

"I highly doubt that's why you came by, but thanks."

Apparently there would be no time for small talk or easing into this. "No, it's not why I came by." She drew in a big breath and held it for a count of five. When she exhaled, he still hadn't moved. He stood staring at her, waiting for her to make the first move. She didn't blame him, after the way they'd left things before. He deserved answers.

No one was blameless in what had happened, not him and certainly not her. But someone had to make the first step toward at least being able to forgive each other, even if that only made it possible for them to move forward in their own lives on separate tracks.

Stalling was not going to make this any easier. "I came by to apologize for dropping that bomb on you and then shutting you out. I shouldn't have told you about the miscarriage that way."

"Shouldn't have told me about it that way or shouldn't have told me at all?"

Sam had never pulled punches when there was truth to be found. It was one of the reasons she had believed the divorce had been the best idea in the end, when he'd simply signed the paperwork without ever asking her a single question.

"Shouldn't have told you that way. And before you think otherwise, I never told anyone about the baby or about the miscarriage. The only people who know are the ones who helped me at the hospital, them and my doctor. But even Flo doesn't know. It wasn't something I wanted to share with anyone until I talked to you, and then when the end came, I didn't want to talk to anyone."

"I see."

Her part was done here then. She wasn't going to stand around and continue to apologize if he wasn't going to give anything back but benign responses.

"I'm sorry for taking your time. I'm sure you have things to do, with Ethan being gone. I'll leave."

"I've never known you to not win an argument." He pushed off from the workbench. "Remember when I wanted the jean couch and you wanted faux suede? You brought home swatches of fabric, boots with the same material, and even found a pair of pants that were a close match, just to get me used to loving the feel of that fabric. And in the end we got your couch because it was what you wanted."

Where was he going with this? They weren't arguing, so there was nothing to win. She answered him anyway. "It was a good couch."

"It was. I admit that now, and I thoroughly enjoyed our time on it, especially when you wore the pants and the two things pretty much became Velcro and you had to have me help you off the couch."

She almost snickered, but that would have been inappropriate. "Where are you going with this? I said I was sorry. You're not saying the same, and I doubt either of us have time to run down memory lane. I just wanted to clear up any misunderstanding. We'll see each other at the wedding next weekend, and possibly at parties, since we have mutual friends. I don't want it to be terribly uncomfortable."

"Yet you're not exactly comfortable right now." He took a step toward her, and it took all she had not to back away. The best thing to do would be to turn and leave. She'd said her piece, and now it was time to go.

"No, I'm not, and that's why I'm leaving. I hope you have a good life, Sam. I appreciate you keeping the miscarriage info to yourself until I had time to tell my friends myself. While I know you weren't there, I'm sure the thought of what was lost didn't make it any easier to handle all these years later. Especially with the way it was dropped on you. I hope you had someone to talk to."

"You're always so damn understanding and just

73

patiently waiting for someone to give you something. Why do you do that?" He stood straight and stalked two steps closer to her.

"What?" Her hand had been on the knob to the door, but she couldn't leave him after that statement. "What the hell is that supposed to mean?"

"It means that when we were married, you gave me everything, you made all the gestures, did the majority of the chores, lived like I was the center of your universe. I thought you were too fragile to handle the reality of the war, so I made a decision to not tell you because I thought I was protecting you. I knew you'd be there when I got back because that was the kind of person you were. I figured I'd calmly explain it was better that I not write, with how ugly it was, and you'd accept my weak-ass excuses and forgive me, and we'd go on to live happily ever after."

He took another step, but she was now rooted to the ground with no way to escape his intense gaze.

"And then you weren't there. I came home ready to tell you that maybe I'd been wrong, ask you to forgive me and go on just like we had been before, but you left me with no explanation, no reason, no forwarding address. If you don't think I tried to find you, then you're sorely mistaken. I did my damndest, but no one would tell me anything. None of them knew you. Hell, they hadn't even known you'd left, until I told them."

"You make me sound like a wallflower or a weed that no one noticed."

"No, what I'm telling you is that you never expected anything from people and I think that's exactly what you got. I'm not saying it's fair, but I'm laying it out there. And then the one time you really needed someone, you didn't even reach out to your own mother."

One more step and he'd be in her personal space. "I handled it."

"Did you? Or did you just bury it?" He took that step and brushed a strand of hair back from her face. "Did you bury it and think it was just one more thing you had to endure? I know your dad left when you were young, and everyone else but you was happy about it, so you didn't tell anyone how sad you were. We talked about that over a bottle of wine one night. I remembered and promised myself I would never leave you. Then I did anyway, and I could kick myself for hurting you, for leaving you to deal with everything on your own. For simply reinforcing that you had no one to lean on."

He cupped her jaw, his long fingers curling around under the bun at the back of her neck, and he broke her with the gesture.

Between sobs she told him that Flo would have been there for her. "I know it, but she had just married my stepfather, and I didn't want to ruin their wedded bliss. It was easier to say that things just didn't work out and go on as if that were the truth."

"But in the end it wasn't easier." He pulled her to him, wrapping her in his muscled arms. With her stature and build she was enveloped by him, totally cocooned in his embrace. She'd thought she'd never feel this safe again in her whole life.

She cried some more until he lifted her chin.

"I loved you, Jocelyn, more than I had thought possible. I was hollow when I came home to our apartment and you were gone. I thought it was all my fault, and maybe you had realized what a selfish bastard I was, so you left. I never would have intentionally made you go through what you went through by yourself."

She swiped a hand under her eye and sniffled. "I know that now. Thank you for telling me, though." She rested her head on his chest, knowing that soon enough she'd be stepping out of his arms and into her own life without him. She clutched the T-shirt front. "Can we at least be friends after this? I don't want to have to walk on the other side of the street, just to avoid burdening you."

His sigh ruffled the hair on her crown. "I don't know if I can do that."

She stiffened, trying to pull away, but he held on tighter, running his hand up and down her back.

"Let me rephrase. I don't think I want to do that." He kissed the top of her head, sending warmth trickling through her body. "I want to try again, if you'll have me. We can date, if you want, start fresh, but I want you back. Even with us not talking over the last few days, knowing you were in the area was enough to make me happier than I've been in years. I want a chance to see if we can recapture what we had, and it's not going to work if I let you put me in the 'friend' box."

Her body remained stiff, but now it was in shock. He wanted her back? He wanted to start over again? But how, with all the water they had gushing under their bridge?

"Same old Jocelyn, thinking too much and worrying if what I say is true. It is, sweetheart. And to get us started, how about this?"

He ran one hand over her head then down her neck

as he pulled her mouth up to his. Little kisses peppered along her cheeks and jaw until she closed her eyes and inhaled the scent of him, the scent of home. He kissed her eyelids, then moved to her ears and down her neck.

Gripping his back, she held on and let her body flow into whatever he wanted. A small part of her felt she should be more cautious and not forget that they'd hurt each other before and could do it again. She told that part to shut the hell up as she felt herself being lifted up onto the workbench and seated with Sam standing between her spread legs.

He continued kissing her as his hand snaked along her neckline and his fingers dipped into her leotard. Her breasts ached, the tips straining for his touch, his mouth, his breath. He slid the straps down and gave her what she was craving. She muffled her cry, fully aware they were in a shop that maybe had no people in it but there were neighbors.

"Maybe we shouldn't do this out here." She tapped Sam's shoulder.

He glanced up at her with a smile. "Mmmm."

She laughed for the first time in a while, her heart light. "I mean it. It's been ten years. The least you could do is offer me a bed."

He pulled the leotard back over her breasts with a chuckle. "I'll go you one better—how about a very special table that has some very special memories? Then we can move to the bed."

"You don't still have that thing."

"I most certainly do. Let me show you." He lifted her in his arms. She snuggled up against him and sighed. When she'd first seen Sam at the studio, she was sure she did not want him to return at all, and now she was halfway to wanting to exchange rings again. The future would tell her exactly how things would work out, but she was ready and in it for the long haul after all. She wouldn't give up so easily this time, because she knew she was not alone.

Getting into the house wasn't easy, since Sam wouldn't put her down, and she had to reach over to open the back door. But they did manage to get in without hitting her head.

Sure enough, he had the table.

He laid her on the polished oak surface, taking up where he'd left off. Beneath him, she writhed, her blood pounding in her ears like a song of coming home. He used his lips and tongue to bring her to the brink before helping her wiggle out of her clothes. But then he had on too many clothes. She giggled, helping him get out of his work boots, and watched in breathless anticipation when he pulled his shirt over his head by gripping the back of the neck. The view of his muscled stomach and lightly haired chest made her legs quiver. She was grateful she was already sitting on the edge of the table.

Then he covered her, his hands everywhere, his mouth trailing along behind in delicious torture. Finally his hands found her core and brought her all the way over the edge. She came apart in his hand, and then he brought her back together with soft kisses and murmured words of love. They'd lost so many years, but tonight was the beginning of something new and yet a continuation of something that would never get old. She trailed her fingers over his stomach, gripping his shoulders when she looked him in the eye. "Inside, now."

"Yes, ma'am."

And they made love like they used to but with a new added layer of love and maturity. When it was over, Sam picked up his pants from the floor and fished something out of the back pocket.

"I pulled these out of my safe when I thought maybe we might have a chance. I was going to put them back after last night, but I just couldn't do it yet." He produced the engagement ring she'd left behind and his own wedding band. "I'm putting mine back on, but it's up to you when you put yours on. I'll give it to you for safekeeping, along with my heart. You just let me know when you're ready."

"I love you, Sam," she said, not trying to hide anything, knowing he had always been the one.

When he tried to hand her the ring, she turned her left hand over and stuck it out with her fingers spread wide. "It doesn't belong in my palm."

Sam searched her eyes, and he seemed to find all the love and hope she had stored up for years behind a wall she had finally let crumble. He put the ring on her finger and kissed her, sealing the deal for real this time.

Misty Simon

Designs on a Dame

by

Misty Simon

Chapter One

The big comfy chair in the library was not big enough to handle the emotions reeling through Adele Dame at the moment. She laid the letter she'd just received on the end table and paced along the perimeter of all the lovely books. She stopped in front of a prominently displayed book, clenching her hand into a fist to keep herself from ripping it off the shelf and throwing it to the floor. First and foremost, she was a logical person, and what would feel good right this instant might be hard to explain later without getting some sidelong glances.

Stalking back over to the end table, she picked up the letter instead. "So sorry, love," she read. "I was going through a rough period, and you helped me through that. I can't thank you enough or apologize eloquently enough for the way I treated you. My therapist felt it was best for me to close doors on past hurts I've caused, so that I might move forward." She slapped the letter against her thigh. "Move forward! The nerve!"

"What's up, chicky?" Her friend Chelsea, one of the owners of the inn Adele managed in the small town of Kissinger, Pennsylvania, stood in the doorway with her hands tucked into her pockets.

Adele tried to remember she should be happy that at least it wasn't Jack who'd found her, as it would

83

rehash a period of her employment here that had been rocky.

Sighing, Adele deflated into the chair. "It's nothing."

"Sure it is, if you're sighing and stomping. What's that?" She pointed at the poisonous piece of paper clutched in Adele's hand.

If it had been Jack, he would have just snatched the thing to see for himself. Adele appreciated that Chelsea would ask. Jack wasn't a bad boss, but they'd worked together long enough to be like brother and sister in some aspects. Friendship had happened between her and Chelsea since the other woman had married Jack and moved in with them, but they had not yet reached the sibling kind of relationship she had with the Jack.

Crumpling the paper in her hand, she aimed it at the fireplace to her left.

"Wait!" Chelsea said, coming farther into the room. "What the heck is going on? You're one of the happiest people I know, no matter what crap guests throw at you, but you look ready to spit nails right now, hon. Before you throw that, whatever it is, why don't you tell me what's going on?"

Adele growled, "Because it's not even worth the breath it would take to explain it."

Sitting in the chair on the other side of the fireplace, Chelsea gave her a doubtful look. "I'm thinking, with the pent-up anger you have going on there, it's worth something or you wouldn't be so pissed. Come on, Adele, we're friends. Lay it on me. You've been there for me over the last few months. In my heart, you're more like a sister than a friend."

Adele blew out another breath. Obviously it was

bothering her, or she wouldn't be ready to scream the inn down around her. Calming herself, she spoke softly so as not to really let that scream out. "Okay. I'm not going to ask you to keep this from Jack. However, I will warn you that it's not something we agreed on when it happened."

"So it's a letter from the asshole who promised you the moon and then never looked back when his book was done."

There shouldn't be a smile on her face, Adele thought, but that's exactly what she felt stretching her cheeks and baring her teeth. "I like that. He was an asshole."

"Of course, he was," Chelsea said matter-of-factly. "I hope you've never doubted the guy was a class-A asshole, actually, from what I've heard from you and Jack. And for the record, if he ever tries to make another reservation here, I'll be the first one to tell him we have no rooms available for his kind."

Adele laughed. "That's not exactly how the service industry works."

Chelsea harrumphed and tucked her legs up under her on the chair. "It does here, and we have enough people booking that we're talking about adding some cabins onto the property for the tourists that should be coming in with the Civil War reenactments the town council has been discussing. It was a good idea on your part, and Jack is totally on board with it. So yeah, there'd be no room for him at all." The satisfied look on Chelsea's face went a long way toward calming Adele. She had been an idiot to trust the guy, yes, but one mistake didn't make her an idiot forever. If nothing else, it had at least made her promise herself she'd never make that same mistake again.

"You're absolutely right."

"So can I read the note?"

With a twist of her wrist, Adele flipped the crumpled paper to Chelsea. The other woman smoothed it out on her thigh, started reading, and then whistled. "Wow, this guy is a bigger piece of work than I thought. What did he do, drag out the thesaurus so he could sound smart while he was doing something dumb?"

The giggle that escaped Adele was not professional, but she wasn't being a professional at the moment, she was being a woman, and that was just as important. Sometimes she had to remind herself of that.

"Thanks. I feel better." At Chelsea's raised eyebrow, Adele added, "No, really. Much better. I just wasn't expecting to hear from him ever again. It's not like I was holding a torch or keeping a candle lit in the window for him, but this took me off guard."

Chelsea handed the paper back. "I was wrong. You should totally throw that piece of trash in the fire."

Adele crumpled it up again into a small ball, threw it on the fire, and they both watched as it burned. Turning to Chelsea, Adele crossed her legs. "So what brought you in, other than my yelling?"

"Oh, right. Jack wanted me to tell you that the guys who were supposed to be here to finish the addition never showed. He'd like you to get in touch with Nate."

****

"Logan, can you take the call on three? I've got a problem child that's going to take a little time."

Logan West nodded to his brother Nate and picked up the phone, hitting the appropriate button before answering, "This is Logan. How can I help you?"

"Hi, Logan. Your guys didn't show up, and I thought I'd call to see what happened."

He'd know that voice anywhere. Adele Dame was the woman who essentially ran the Barton Inn owned by Jack Barton and his wife Chelsea. She was fun but no nonsense when it came to the addition their company, Due West, had contracted to finish before the wedding of Dex and Zoe. The addition was for Jack and his new family. Previously, Jack and Adele and the cook, Frank, had lived on the third floor for years with no space issues. But now, with the addition of Chelsea and her daughter Mazzy as permanent fixtures in the house, things had gotten crowded.

"Are you sure?" He leaned back in his chair and tapped a pencil on the desk. "They should have been there an hour ago." He glanced at the clock to make sure his timing was right and realized it actually should have been almost ninety minutes ago.

"I'm aware when they should have been here. But they aren't here. Can you please call and find out what the holdup is? This job needs to be done in less than a week because of the wedding."

She didn't exactly sound pissed, but her voice was stern. Not someone he'd want to mess with at the moment.

"Sure, sure. I'll go get them myself. I sent them to do a quick fix on Mrs. Worcester's house before heading out your way. Maybe they found more than they were expecting. I'll be out there myself in a few."

"Fine. Thank you. I'll expect you shortly."

All business, all the time. That was Adele. His sister-in-law Claudia had made a few noises about him asking Adele out, but he was not going to touch that invitation. For one thing, dating any friend of Claudia's would be a mistake. If anything bad happened, it would automatically be his fault. For two, Adele was not a beer-and-pizza kind of girl with some fooling around to round out the night. She had "permanent" written all over her, and he was a temporary kind of guy.

They hung up agreeing to meet at the inn, and he grabbed his coat off the rack by the door.

"Can you hold on a minute, Therese?" Nate said into the phone, then pushed the mute button. "Where are you headed off to in such a hurry?"

"Adele called. The guys didn't show up, and she is not a happy camper."

"Damn. This is a big job, and those cabins Jack called about would be even bigger in the spring. We can't afford to screw this up."

"I know. That's why I'm heading out."

Nate smiled. "Hey, maybe while you're there you could butter her up by offering to take her out for drinks, like Claudia keeps suggesting."

"God, you too? Not happening. The woman is nice, I'll give you that, but not my type. If we get into trouble, I'll offer her a discount, but it's coming out of your cut."

Banging the office door shut behind him, Logan jumped into his company truck and headed toward Mrs. Worcester's house. The guys better have come across something huge, or Adele was not going to be the only one using a sharp tone.

****

An hour later, Adele paced back and forth in the library. The note from the asshole had long ago burned to ashes, but Logan still hadn't shown up. There had better be a very good reason for this and for not contacting her in the interim, she fumed.

Another circuit and she was getting tired of the same scenery. But she didn't want to go into the kitchen because then she'd have to talk to Frank. Even though the letter was a pile of ashes, it was still fresh in her mind.

Her hand fisted. It shouldn't matter to her at all. He was years ago. No, she hadn't dated since then, but she hadn't been asked, either, and she hadn't sought anyone out. She had the inn, which was picking up business at a steady pace, increasing their guest count on an almost weekly basis.

Hosting the weddings had been a sheer stroke of genius. They had the landscape for the most beautiful backdrop imaginable. They had plans to pave more of the backyard with sand-colored stone come the spring, and then they would begin work on the cabins. Her excitement about the cabins hadn't decreased even a smidge since Jack had first brought them up about eight weeks ago.

The town council had announced plans to host a reenactment weekend, and the inn sat right in the middle of a field where a battle had raged. The land had been in Jack's family for years, but the battle had not been a big one in the history books, just here in the area. More people were becoming interested in the history, though, and even more wanted ghost tours of the area.

They wouldn't be as popular as Gettysburg, to the south, but they could hold their own. And more tourists meant more guests at the inn. She and Jack had even discussed hosting their own ghost weekend if it would bring people in. But when they brought the people in, they needed a place for them to stay. Other bed and breakfasts existed in the area, along with a few smaller chain hotels, but this could be really big. Ever the savvy businessman, Jack didn't want to miss out on it.

So they were building cabins. And if Adele had her way, she would get a cabin of her own and run that portion of things while Chelsea and Jack ran the inn itself. She didn't feel pushed out; in fact, Chelsea almost always deferred to her. But Adele could tell the other woman was fairly itching to get more involved with the day-to-day business. This would be the closest thing to running her own inn that Adele could imagine without actually leaving. She so did not want to leave.

This was the perfect compromise. Or it would be if the guys on that crew were more reliable than the current ones. Adele looked at the grandfather clock standing in the corner. She'd successfully managed to distract herself for almost another fifteen minutes. Logan had another five before she was forced to put in another call and actually talk to Nate this time.

As she passed the front window for the twenty-fifth time, a truck rolled along the long driveway leading from the main road. Finally.

Meeting him in the parking lot was better for her blood pressure than continuing to pace in the library. He was going to get an earful—a professional earful, but an earful nonetheless.

Or at least that was the plan when she marched up to the driver's side of the truck as it parked around back. Logan was alone, not another man in sight. Obviously no work was getting done today.

Logan stepped out of the truck, all legs and broad shoulders. She took a step back so as not to crowd him. She'd never realized how truly big the man was. No little flower herself, with all her curves and her plump figure, she was taken aback by the sheer size of him. Heaven help her if he didn't blot out the sun when she stood this close to him.

"Sorry it took so long," Logan offered as he closed the truck door behind him. "I promise the guys will be out here this afternoon."

He sounded weary. Was he embarrassed? Tired? None of that was her business. Getting the inn done on time was her only business.

"May I ask what happened?" she asked in her best professional voice as she crossed her arms over her chest and stilled her tapping foot.

"Sure. Do you have about ten minutes?" He raised his gaze to hers and looked as weary as he sounded.

She backed up another step. "Frank has a pot of coffee always going, if you need a jump for the afternoon."

"I appreciate it, but I don't have time. The job the guys were working before yours this morning went haywire when one guy fell off a ladder, another guy's wife called him in labor three weeks early, and then the client stumbled over an extension cord in an area where she was specifically asked to stay out of and the third and final guy had to run her to the emergency room for a possible broken ankle."

"Wow." Not her most intelligent response, but she had no other words and felt like a heel for being ready to tear into him.

"Yeah, well, they say these things come in threes,

right? So that should be my three."

"Right." God, she sincerely hoped the letter wasn't the beginning of her three and this was the second.

"I'd better get back. Nate and I will be out later this afternoon with my dad and at least one other guy. There's not a ton left to do, but with the wedding this weekend we want to make sure it's all done right. The wedding will be a big boost for your business, and it potentially is one for ours, too."

"Of course." She took another step back, aware that one more would have her standing in her own flower beds.

"Thanks for being so nice, Adele. Not everyone is as accepting. I told Nate you would understand, being in business yourself." He hopped back in the truck, rolling down the window and sticking his elbow out. "We'll be about three hours. You don't have anyone staying right now, do you?"

"No."

"Good. Okay. We might be here into the night, if that's okay. Do you think we're far enough away from Mazzy to not disturb her if we work past her bedtime?"

She almost took that last step back and stopped herself with her foot barely lifted. "Um, no, it should be fine. Jack and Chelsea and Mazzy will be out to dinner tonight with Jack's sister, so they aren't planning on being back until after nine. If things stay as usual, then Mazzy should be asleep before they come in the door. I'll have them put her in my room if necessary."

"Great. Thanks. See you in a few." He rolled the window back up and sent her a brief wave as he cranked the engine. Placing his arm across the back of the seats, he twisted to back up efficiently. He waved to her again as he took off down the lane.

She stood there for another minute, not sure what to make of that exchange or the thoughts that were flying around her head right now.

The letter. It had to be the letter and the turmoil she had been thrown into after reading it that made her notice the slight shadow of a beard on Logan, the way he stood over a foot taller than her, the sheer breadth of his shoulders, the way his hair gleamed in the midmorning winter sun, the size of his hands, and the way his jeans fit. It was a lot to take in during such a short conversation. But somehow her mind had catalogued it all and tucked it into her brain along with the way her heart had stuttered just a little bit with his concern for Mazzy.

****

Logan spent the next two hours putting out fires while Nate got the necessary tools together for their afternoon of working double time. Just like old times, their mom packed them dinner as if they all still lived at home. She kissed their dad, Nate, and Logan as she sent them out the door and told them to be careful.

Logan carried a to-go cup from a local diner as he approached the trucks. Nate jumped into his truck, and their dad climbed into Logan's truck. In the driver's side. Logan rolled his eyes as he ran around the hood to open the passenger's side door. "Got to take the wheel, huh, old man?"

"I drive better than you do, and I won't be distracted by anything walking along the sidewalk in a skirt." Jeff West winked at Logan as he turned the key in the ignition.

Logan didn't roll his eyes again because his dad

would see him and probably pop him in the arm. But mentally he did roll them. Yes, he enjoyed looking at the fairer sex. He enjoyed taking them out, holding them, and even going a little farther than that with a few of them. But, at the end of the day, he was perfectly capable of keeping his mind on business when business was at hand.

A very clear picture of Adele this afternoon popped into his head, and he shooed it away. He blamed Nate for the way he'd noticed her today. Logan had worked for weeks at the inn, said hi to her, and conferred with her over a number of things regarding the addition. He'd noticed before that she was pretty, in an understated way, and had curves galore, but he'd always seen her as a business associate. Except today had been different, with her standing so close, her hair in a messy knot with wisps floating in the light wind that had kicked up. He'd had to hastily shove his hands into his pockets when he found himself wanting to reach out and tuck the strands behind her ears.

He was not going to get involved with one of Claudia's friends. Absolutely not. And not only was she Claudia's friend, she was also Zoe's friend and May's and Jocelyn's and Paige's. There was no more perfect recipe for disaster, and he was not falling into that trap. Give him some barfly any day over a woman who had "permanent" stamped all over her.

And the to-go cup was filled with a treat he hoped would smooth the irritation she'd obviously been feeling earlier. It was better than offering her a steep discount for something they were trying to fix.

"Where are you at?" Jeff asked, turning down the lane to the inn.

Logan jerked himself back to the moment. "Right here, going over the plans and what has to be completed."

His dad smirked. "Right. I hear that Dame girl is a looker and that your brother is trying to get you to ask her out. I'll have to see for myself."

Oh, Lord. He just wanted to do his job and get out of here. Now there was a new layer. He'd have to make sure to keep his eyes to himself and be on guard so he didn't get caught trying to see if she really did have a small beauty mark at the curve of her collarbone. He'd had brief thoughts of whether or not that was a sweet spot for her earlier. No more of that, or he'd be in a world of trouble.

Chapter Two

The kitchen was in an uproar, or at least Frank, the cook, was.

"You're just now telling me the guys will be here over dinner? I don't have anything thawed out."

Adele kept her tongue in her cheek to stop the snicker from tumbling out of her mouth. The blocky former serviceman took his kitchen seriously. She thought they'd just throw a few sandwiches together and call it a meal, but Frank obviously had other ideas.

"What do I have that I can make?" he mumbled to himself as he yanked open the refrigerator and stuck his head inside. He poked his head around the door. "Don't just stand there. Get me some pepperoni out of the freezer in the back room."

"What are you talking about? Why am I getting pepperoni, and why do you say it like I should know?"

"Because we're having Sicilian pizza. That's why. And I need the pepperoni. Now run along." He dismissed her with a ball of mozzarella cheese and jar of his homemade pizza sauce in his hands.

Well, apparently she had her marching orders.

****

True to his word, Logan showed up at three with a crew. He also had a tall hot chocolate with extra whipped cream.

"You're not a coffee kind of girl, from what I

hear."

Who had he heard that from? Who had he asked? She supposed any of the women she knew and whom he was friends with could have filled him in. But what had they thought when he'd asked?

"Thanks," she said before she forgot, in her haze of chocolate love. Frank made a mean hot chocolate, but Mercy down at the Corner Cafe made it just a tiny bit better. Of course, she'd never told Frank that and never would...

"My pleasure."

And he looked like he actually meant it. He could not be flirting with her.

It was a ridiculous thought to even think much less entertain. Business. She had to think business. "Thanks for coming by. If there's anything you need, please don't hesitate to ask. Frank's in the kitchen making dinner for a few hours from now."

"We brought—"

Nate elbowed his brother. "Sounds great, Adele. I'm sure we'll love whatever he cooks up. We'll be in the addition if you need us. The noise will probably be terrific, but I promise we'll try to keep the swearing down as much as possible." Nate walked off after slapping Logan in the back.

"The guy thinks he's hysterical."

"I'm sure he does," Adele responded, with a straight face and one eyebrow raised.

"I think I like that you might not be impressed with his brand of humor." He looked her over from head to toe.

She forced her body not to react with the shiver that wanted to run up her spine.

"Go be not impressed in the addition," she said, shooing him with her free hand. "We're behind, and I'd like to get back on schedule."

He gave her a lopsided grin that pinged at her lady parts. Good Lord, down, girl! The salute, though, and the "Yes, ma'am. Right away, ma'am" finally caused her to chuckle and the other side of his sensual mouth kicked up.

She turned away before she could get sucked into his twinkling eyes. She fanned herself discreetly as he walked away whistling.

"Hey, Nate, I'm the funny one this time, man. Take that and stick it."

****

Back in the day, when Nate had just graduated high school and Logan wasn't far behind, Logan, Nate, and Jeff were the only crew for Due West. His dad would bring in a helper here and there as needed, but he rarely took on jobs that were beyond what he and his sons could handle. Logan had not always loved the work, as he would have preferred to be out looking for girls, taking girls out, or escorting girls home, with a basketball game or two thrown in for good measure, but now he loved the work. They got to do so many different kinds of projects, from fixing roofs to fixing sinks, from pouring concrete to enclosing porches, and a number of other construction jobs in between. With living in a small town, it wasn't as if there were a ton of new houses to build. It was more that the stately old ladies needed to be fixed up and cared for as they aged. But people liked new outbuildings, too. The famed new She Sheds had kept them in business up to their ears over the beginning of fall, and they had orders for even more this coming spring.

Following along behind Nate, Jeff and Logan trooped through a discreet door set in the wall next to the coat closet in the downstairs hall and entered the addition. They'd done a good job, as far as Logan was concerned. The living area had all the hookups for any kind of electronics Jack might want. Behind that was a dining room, a private laundry room, and a sitting room. Upstairs they had three bedrooms and two bathrooms. Most of the rooms were nearly done. The siding was today's project and had to be completed as soon as possible. The scaffolding was against the house already, since some of the top sections had been placed. And all of the sections had been cut. It was going to be a matter of getting them up and securing them.

Then once that was done they had interior work to keep them busy for the rest of the evening. The dining room had built-in shelves that needed to be set and then molding put around the ceiling. It was mostly finishing work, but it still had to be done.

"Are we ready to get to work?" Jeff asked.

"Yep," Logan and Nate chorused.

"Okay, then. And the faster we get this done, the faster we get to eat something besides the tuna fish sandwiches your mom packed for us. And maybe that pretty lady will sit down with us for dinner. You were right, Nate. She is a looker, and nice to boot." Jeff winked at Logan as he added, "I think it would be a good thing if you went for her, Logan. If she'd have you, that is."

"That's what I said, but I don't know," Nate said. "She didn't laugh at my joke about the swearing. It could be she doesn't have the sense of humor Logan seems to think makes the girls come to the yard."

Logan flicked the back of his brother's ear. "She might not have laughed at your joke, but she laughed at mine, big guy." And he walked past him, out through the back door in the laundry room to the yard where all the siding was stacked neatly in a large box just waiting to finish up this beauty of an addition.

Maybe he would get to have dinner with Adele. Not that he wanted to start anything with her, but she was more than met the eye. He thought he might like that about her.

****

Dinner had gone over well. The guys ate almost an entire huge pizza on their own. As much as she had tried to leave them alone in the dining room to enjoy Frank's creation, they were having none of that. They refused to eat unless both Frank and Adele sat with them at the big oak table usually reserved for guests.

What followed was an hour of joking, laughing, and teasing. Nate and Logan had a great relationship, going after each other over and over again verbally, while their dad filtered in a remark every few minutes. She and Frank laughed at their antics, knowing that she, Jack, and Frank had the same kind of relationship.

When it was time for them to go back to work, she helped with the dishes, against Frank's wishes.

"You cooked and served. The least I can do is help with the dishes. I didn't have to do anything tonight but laugh."

"It was good, wasn't it?" Frank handed her the baking dish to set in the sudsy water.

"It was." She dunked the dish, then got to scrubbing.

"That Logan couldn't seem to keep his eyes off you." Frank handed her a spatula, and she grabbed it without looking at him.

Sure that a blush crept up from her neckline, she dunked the spatula in the water, concentrating on it like it was the answer to every question in the universe. "I wouldn't know. I was having too much fun interacting with everyone. I love our guests, but we don't always get to interact with them that way."

"Come on." Frank nudged her with his shoulder. "You can't tell me you didn't notice him looking at you."

"I didn't, and I doubt you did, either."

"I might not be young, but my eyes work just fine, and so do my ears. He tried to talk directly to you a couple times, and yet you talked to the whole table. Did he make you nervous?"

The teasing was to be expected, but when she wasn't sure what she felt, teasing was not exactly welcome. She'd have to play it off, though, or Frank would become suspicious. And a suspicious Frank could get her into all kinds of trouble. She didn't think there was a rule against dating someone who worked for Jack; she'd never asked. Yet she didn't want to make the mistake of even entertaining the thought for a moment. Because while it might not be a bad thing, it could be awkward if she suggested something and Logan turned her down flat. He was very much a confirmed bachelor, and she didn't see him changing that for anyone, especially not her.

"He didn't make me nervous. He made me giddy when they said the outside was almost done and they're going to be able to come in under the timeframe.

They're coming back tomorrow with all their guys to finish it out." She put the spatula in the drainer to the left of the sink. "Maybe you'd better go hunt through the freezer for something for tomorrow. I think it would be nice to have a lunch for all of them."

"Nice subject change." He tugged on the end of hair that had escaped the knot on top of her head.

"Well, you weren't going to do it, so I had to. There's nothing more to talk about regarding Logan. He's a nice enough guy, but I'm not his type."

She kept telling herself that, even as she prepared for bed, talking to herself in the mirror around her toothbrush and as she brushed out her hair.

She didn't know how much she had talked herself into the idea that he was completely out of her league. No matter the answer, her subconscious did not listen. She dreamed about him all night long.

****

Another day, and the work was done. Two days before the wedding of Dex and Zoe, and finally he and his dad and Nate stood back from the finished project and slapped each other on the back.

"Looks good, there, guys. We still do good work together." Jeff stuck his hands in the pockets of his workman's pants and admired their handiwork.

Jack came out to stand with them. "I can't thank you all enough for getting this done. If I had known how extensive it was going to be, I would have waited for spring."

"Nah, it's good to have work year-round," Jeff said. "And in the spring we'll be working on those cabins of yours."

"Yes, I think they'll be a great thing to have for the

inn. With all the tourists we expect to have coming in, we should benefit handsomely from them. And Adele was just saying she has a writing group interested in using them for a writing retreat. I'm sure they won't be the only ones, when it's all said and done. You guys do amazing work. It's all I can do to get the sink unclogged."

The men all laughed, including Logan, but his mind was running around the fact that his excuse for seeing Adele on a nearly daily basis was no longer going to be his to use. And since it was December, the spring seemed too far away to wait to see her again.

Although he would see her this weekend at the combination bachelor and bachelorette party, and then the next day at the wedding. Maybe he could cook up something to draw her interest in those thirty-six hours.

He'd told himself he wasn't interested in her, dredged up the excuse that she was a friend of Claudia's and he didn't want to be blamed if something went wrong, even pulled up the fact that he was the last standing bachelor and didn't want to change that status. But none of it seemed to be working. Sitting with her last night over dinner had made him wish they were around the table with his mom, too. While it had given him pause for a moment, since he'd never in his life taken anyone home, it had felt right.

Looking up, he caught a glimpse of her coming around the corner of the house to do her own inspection. The words to ask her out hovered on his tongue. He just couldn't seem to get them to come out. What if she said no? He'd have to come up with something for the wedding.

Chapter Three

One more day until the pre-wedding party, and Logan had come up with nothing good. Was he reaching outside of his league, and that's why it was so hard to come up with a way to ask Adele out? Normally he just said, "Hey, want to go grab something to eat?" and the rest followed from there, but something about her made him feel that his A-game might not be enough. He closed his eyes for just a moment in disbelief. It shouldn't be this hard, dammit. She was just a woman, he was just a man. What was the big deal?

When he opened his eyes, Claudia was standing in front of him with a white-paper-wrapped piece of heaven in her hands.

"Oh, please tell me that's what I think it is," he said, smiling.

"What, this thing?" She waved the package around and the unmistakable smell of onions and fresh baked bread wafted across the desk.

"Oh, man, tell me that's not for Nate. I swear I'll take you to the Caribbean and buy you your own island if you'll leave that loser and run away with me."

Claudia laughed at their running joke. "I'm not going anywhere. Now that I have Nate right where I want him, I'm certainly not going to give him up, even for you, cutie."

"Not even if I said something really nice about your beautiful new haircut?"

Claudia touched the ends of the shorter hair and smiled at him. "Even then. Nate already noticed and said it looks beautiful."

"One-upped again. How am I going to be satisfied with anyone less than you?"

She laughed and sat on the edge of his desk. "I know exactly who you could go after, but you aren't following my orders. Why is that?"

He didn't know if he was ready to have this conversation. Yet something told him he probably wasn't going to get out of it. He could simply tell her he planned on asking Adele out. It might work. Then again, he wasn't sure he wanted anyone to know before Adele did, and maybe not at all if she said no.

Shrugging instead of answering her, he said, "I don't think she'd go out with me, and you know me, Confirmed Bachelor."

She narrowed her eyes at him. "I'm not sure I'm as convinced of that as when I walked in."

"I don't know what you're talking about. Now can I have my sandwich? I'm starving. It's hard work drawing up these sketches for those cabins Jack wants put in and giving them all the amenities he's looking for."

At his smile, she put the sandwich down and went to the door of the office. She didn't leave until she'd given him one last look over her shoulder. "I'm keeping an eye on you."

"Of course you are. How else will you remind yourself daily of what you gave up to be with that dork Nate?"

She laughed again and left, finally. Chewing his sandwich, he brought his sketch pad of paper back in front of him and wrote out a few more ideas on how exactly he could get Adele alone. Nothing was sparking. He might just have to wing it like he'd always done. It was dumb to try to plan out something like this anyway. He wrote down one more idea, then a couple more as he finished off his hoagie. Something would come to him.

****

The ladies had taken over the speakeasy for the night. Adele watched from the old bar in the basement as Zoe opened gift after gift from her friends and sister. They'd all gone together to get her a cabin at the beach for the weekend after the first of the year. She and Dex had decided to wait until their niece was a little older and the house more settled before they took a full-fledged honeymoon. This way they could at least get away for a weekend in between so they could be just the two of them. Adele understood the need for that because of living with everyone here at the inn.

Zoe laughed at a gift, bringing Adele's attention back to the room. "I don't know that I need all this!" Zoe kept bringing lingerie piece after lingerie piece out of the huge stuffed bag on the wooden table. "Claudia, you're going to be the death of me."

"I love you, and I'm so happy you decided to stop being so damn stubborn about what a great guy Dex is, so I think he deserves a treat, too, for putting up with you."

The whole room erupted with laughter. Adele got another bottle of wine from under the bar and uncorked it to fill half-empty glasses.

The innkeeper in her wondered how the guys were doing upstairs in the new living room in the addition as they gave their own gifts and played poker while drinking beer.

Everyone was staying the night, so she didn't worry about who was getting home and how. Though of course she could have drunk, too, she considered herself the designated getting-to-bedder and would pour as long as everyone was drinking and having fun.

They'd started with a magnificent dinner of steak with roasted potatoes, asparagus, and a creamy cheese sauce that was Frank's specialty. Everyone had eaten up in the dining room. Adele hadn't realized until the last minute that with Frank in the kitchen, Adele and Logan were the only ones in the room not paired off. She'd sat next to him, and they'd talked even as she'd been aware of a few sidelong glances in their direction.

As much as he was definitely attractive and fun to be with, though, she was not in the market for a man. And if she felt the need for a rebound guy, after that stupid note from the writer guy, then the last person she would want to get involved with was Nate's brother. No way would they be able to avoid each other when things didn't work out. And she was pretty sure things wouldn't work out. They had fun together, but how much did they really have in common?

She shook her head at herself. It didn't matter. After tomorrow, she probably wouldn't see him again until the spring. By then he would have moved on to the next flavor of the week—probably several times. And she? Well, she might decide to do a little dating here and there now that she'd have more leisure time. Or maybe she'd take one of Jocelyn's Zumba classes.

There were more opportunities for her to get a real social life, with Chelsea here, and maybe it was time for Adele to start taking advantage of some of them.

Games were next on the agenda. Adele was ready with the toilet paper to make brides. So much laughter rang through the room, and it was a really good sound. She loved every single woman down here in this speakeasy and was so happy to have them in her life.

"A toast!" she yelled over the chatter.

"A toast!" everyone yelled back.

"To the best damn bunch of broads this side of the Mississippi!" She raised her glass of cola.

"Here, here!"

****

Logan escorted the last guy up the stairs and into the waiting arms of his girlfriend or wife. The only exception was that Dex was staying in the addition, away from Zoe, who was staying in the bridal suite. Other than that, everyone else had a significant other.

Well, everyone but him and Adele and Frank, he guessed. Frank had gone to bed hours ago, and he'd passed Adele on the stairs a few minutes ago as she escorted a snickering Claudia up the stairs. They shared a smile, and he wondered what she'd do if he knocked on her door before he headed back to his apartment alone. Probably smack him, if she was sober, since she had to get up at the crack of dawn to start prep for the wedding. He was staying at his place because the rooms not used by the wedding party were taken up by out-of-town guests.

He snuck into the kitchen for one last soda before he headed out, only to find Adele washing dishes.

"You doing all these by yourself?" He counted

twenty assorted glasses on the counter, from long-stemmed wine glasses to brandy snifters and beer mugs. A stack of plates, plus pans and silverware, sat on the butcher block in the middle of the kitchen, along with a plate with the remains of the tuxedo cake the guys had enjoyed and another with what was left of a cake covered with bouquets of flowers all over it.

"Oh, Logan, hi." She used her elbow to move some hair off her cheek. Her hands were covered in suds from the sink, the sleeves of her button-down dress shirt were rolled to the middle of her forearms, her hair was slipping out of its ponytail, and a spot of something marred her left cheek. And he'd never wanted to kiss a woman more.

Shit!

"Can I, um, help? I was going to head back to my apartment, but I don't want to leave you with all this by yourself."

"No, you don't have to."

He shoved the sleeves of his sweater up to his elbow and started scraping food into the trash can next to the refrigerator. "I guess I wasn't asking. I'm helping. No way am I going to leave you with all this, when you have to be up at who knows what time tomorrow to get things rolling for the wedding."

Her grateful smile was enough to have him scraping double time and then wrapping up the cakes and stowing them in the refrigerator. They worked in companionable silence for a few moments.

"You bringing anyone to the wedding tomorrow?" he asked on his second trip to the sink with cleaned plates.

"Oh, no. I'll be working, and I don't have anyone I

would have asked anyway."

"So, no boyfriend?" he asked as casually as possible.

She glanced at him out of the corner of her bright eyes. "No, no boyfriend. And you? Who's the girlfriend of the week this week?"

He grabbed his chest dramatically. "You wound me. I haven't dated anyone in months."

"Yeah, right. There's always a new arm candy with you."

"No, really," he said. "No one new. Going solo tomorrow."

"I'm sure you'll find someone to dance with while you're there." She rinsed the last dish and handed it to him.

He never had taken any pleasure in domestic chores, preferring to leave things until he ran out of dishes before he washed anything. But the past hour had been the best he'd had in a long, long time.

"All done. I can't thank you enough. That would have taken a whole lot longer without you, Logan. I really appreciate you sticking around."

And this was where he could ask if they could go out to dinner some night, or hell, he'd come over and wash dishes with her again. How pathetic was that?

But she was ushering him out of the kitchen, turning off lights behind her.

She saw him to the front door. He could have hugged her or touched her hand or something, anything, but he chose not to. How would she take it? They'd just talked about his flavor of the week, and he did not want her to think he was looking to fill the position with her.

"Good night."

"Good night," he said, patting his pockets for his keys. "Damn. I must have left the keys in the living room."

"You know your way." She yawned behind her hand. "I'm going to be a bad host and head up for the night. The door locks behind you, so don't worry about it."

"Okay, good night, then."

"See you tomorrow."

He stood in the hallway like an idiot, watching her trail her hand up the banister to the second floor, wishing those fingers were trailing over him.

He hustled through the house, quietly opening the door to the living room, hoping not to disturb anyone sleeping.

He most certainly was not expecting to find Chelsea sitting on the couch in a robe with a mug of something that steamed up around her pretty face and Jack rubbing her feet.

"Oh, man, I'm sorry. I guess I should have…knocked?" What did you do when you went into another part of a house?

Chelsea laughed. "No worries, Logan. What's up?"

"I, um, forgot my keys."

"And what have you been doing for the last hour? You put everyone in bed over an hour ago. I thought you were heading out then."

"Yeah, that was the plan, but then I found Adele in the kitchen with all those dishes." He shrugged.

Chelsea swung her feet off the side of the couch. "I should go help her. I can't believe I didn't think about that. I'll be back."

Logan stopped her before she could rush off.

"Everything's done and put away."

"Is it now?" Jack stared hard at him, making him almost want to squirm. Almost. It wasn't like he'd done anything wrong. In fact, the very opposite had happened.

"Yep, and now I should get going. Have you seen my keys?"

"I'm pretty sure Nate took them downstairs into the speakeasy when he tried to sneak out to see Claudia. It was his excuse, if I remember correctly."

"Thanks. I'll go look for them and then head out. Tomorrow will come soon enough, and I don't want to be late for the wedding. We have that…" He glanced at Chelsea, not sure if she knew about the dance that Jocelyn had helped them all learn to perform tomorrow after cake was served. "We have that thing to do." He pulled the door open behind him. "Well, see you tomorrow." And he ducked out before anyone could question him.

The speakeasy was on the way back to the front door. Stupid Nate, of course he'd taken the keys. He probably thought it was funny. One quick stop was not going to be a problem, though, and then he'd be home for the night and sleep well for tomorrow. He still hadn't come up with anything to impress Adele enough to make her want to go out with him. He still had time.

****

She might actually beat her best time on her favorite game, and there was no way to save her progress unless she got to the next level. Two more minutes, and then she'd go to bed. After everything that had happened tonight, Adele had needed some time to unwind with her guilty pleasure before heading upstairs. Yes, she had to be up early in the morning, but if she'd gone straight up, she'd still be staring at the ceiling wondering why Logan, who she'd seen in and out of the inn for weeks, was suddenly affecting her like he had while helping her do dishes.

On screen, her little car whizzed around a corner and jumped through a halo that sent her a hundred yards in front of everyone else on the track. She was going to get this trophy on Deranged Mode. She would have done a victory yell, but she didn't want to wake anyone up. She'd save it for tomorrow.

Video games were her guilty pleasure, and one only the people in the house knew about. She was all business most of the time. Yet even she needed an outlet. Racing cars on the sixty-inch TV in the back room off the speakeasy at the inn was the perfect way to deal with how her life was currently playing out.

Pulling to the right, she whipped past a tree, threw a canister out the car window, and cheered when it blew up the car behind her.

"Nice work."

She almost bobbled the controller. She barely kept it in her hand and her eyes on the screen so as not to have to face Logan. There would be enough time for him to laugh at her after she got the trophy.

She careened around a corner, took a sharp right, hitting the brakes to drift, and crossed the finish line with her best time yet. The trophy popped up on the screen—held, of course, by a scantily clad woman who had enough chest that if she were real she'd fall over with every step.

Adele dropped the controller into her lap, still not wanting to face Logan. "I thought you left twenty minutes ago."

"I forgot my keys. I thought they were in Jack's new living room. Seems Nate brought them down here, instead."

She heard a rustle but didn't look over.

"Does this have versus mode? I've wanted to buy it. Almost did, then talked myself out of it because I just couldn't justify it, with winter coming on and jobs slowing down."

Now she did look over at him, to make sure he wasn't making fun of her. He'd pulled up the extra game chair that Jack used when they played Mortal Kombat. His long legs were stretched out in front of him in the low chair, his hands braced on his thighs as he leaned forward, his gaze intent on the screen as the girl jumped up and down with the trophy. Yeah, she definitely would have had to readjust her center of gravity if those breasts were real.

"Over there." Adele raised her controller to gesture to the cabinet on the side of the entertainment center. They had the speakeasy in the basement, a room that Jack had refurbished for guests to feel like they were back during the prohibition years. Warm wood accented the room, tall booths lent privacy, and a wine bar held every kind of local flavor available. A chess board sat on one of the tables and candles graced every table. She'd cleaned up down here, too, after the party, and everything was back in its place. Except Logan shouldn't be here.

This room, though, was hidden around the corner and behind a big weathered-looking door. It was filled with electronics and seven different game systems. Some systems were interactive with the player's body;

with those she played games and even exercised. Other games required hours of play, and some were quick, two-minute games in which she destroyed bubbles. She even had the old-school stuff.

He leaned forward on the chair, grabbed the control, and settled back. "I might not be able to beat you, but I might just give you a run for your money. Justin and I play all the time. Neither of us are as good as you, though."

Studying him, she narrowed her eyes. She knew Claudia's son played games. She had never heard about Logan being a fan. "And you'll be okay with losing?"

"Well, let's not count on that until the race is over. I might have a trick or two up my sleeve." He smiled, and her insides quivered just a little bit. She told them to knock it the heck off.

She hit start. They both chose their vehicles, the type of transmission, and the color. She chose the track, and they were off. He was not bad at this at all. They were neck and neck for the first third of the track. After the first checkpoint, she pulled out in front and rammed him into a wall. He groaned but got right down to business. That groan did something to her insides, and she couldn't help glancing over at him and the way he bit his lip with concentration. He was one of those people who moved the controller from left to right like it would really make any kind of difference. A loud crash happened on screen, jerking her attention back to the game, and she moaned when she realized she'd wrapped her car almost completely around a tree. And he'd shot past her.

His smile was even wider. She vowed there and then that she wasn't going to look at it anymore. She had a game to win.

In the end, he beat her by a half second. He hooted and pumped his fist in the air. Fortunately, he wasn't a jackass about it, which was a nice change from the guys she had played with back in the day, who called her a girl in a sneering voice that meant she sucked because she didn't have that Y chromosome that apparently made them better players. Totally not true.

"That was awesome, thanks." Logan turned to her in his chair, his enthusiasm enough to make her smile back at him.

"You did well."

"Eh, it was luck."

Yeah, that or her distraction with his good looks. She backed away from that thought quickly enough. She'd been having too many of them lately. Making him a rebound guy was wrong. There was no way he would be anything more. She'd never been interested before, and it was only after the letter that she'd noticed him. That was not fair to him.

"I should head up to bed." She rose from her game chair and waited for Logan to do the same.

He stayed where he was. "No time for one more run around the track?" He waved the controller at her. "I know morning is coming soon, but one more won't take too long."

Against her better judgment, she sank back down. "One more. Then I really have to go."

Logan's rich laugh sent a tiny thrill down her spine. She told the bone structure to knock it off and concentrated on beating the pants off him.

Yeah, not exactly an image she should have entertained for even a second, but she still beat him this time. He was a good sport. He did try to talk her into a tie-breaker, though. She turned him down for her own good.

"It's time for me to head up. I'm sure you need your rest to keep all those single ladies dancing tomorrow at the wedding."

She purposely did not look at his face when she said the words, knowing he'd either be smiling, which could melt her bones, or he'd be frowning, which would make her feel like a bitch.

Her dreams were going to be chaotic tonight. She walked him to the door, made sure it locked behind him, then leaned her head against the wood. Why, oh, why did he have to be everything she wanted right when she shouldn't?

Chapter Four

Logan drove home with his radio blasting to drown out his thoughts. She played video games. She was beautiful and fun and intelligent. She was totally out of his league. And she thought he was always on the lookout for the next piece of arm candy.

He couldn't deny the past. He had only been looking for shallow relationships before. But, the future somehow felt different. Adele's face flashed in the front of his mind. Her laughing eyes, her concentration when she was playing the game, her beauty mark at the base of her neck—that he still wanted to taste. They'd had a great time washing dishes, and he hated doing dishes. How did she make everything fun? And how was he going to get her to take him seriously, to see if they could be good together on a more intimate level?

His apartment complex came into view, and he maneuvered into his spot out front. No lights shone in any windows. It must have been later than he'd thought. Looking at the dash clock, he realized he'd driven around for almost an hour. He hadn't been so lost in thought about a woman since his teens. Was that a good thing, or was he building things up with her in his mind to an impossible standard?

Tomorrow was the wedding, and he'd see how it went. If the opportunity presented itself, he'd ask her out once and for all. He'd make sure she knew it was one date that they could both walk away from if it didn't work out. No harm, no hard feelings. Just two people going out for something to eat and to see if there was a connection there, a connection he found himself craving as much as he craved tasting her.

****

The sun was up, and so was Adele. Wishing to be back in bed under the covers didn't make it so. Donning a pair of pants and a sweatshirt, she got to work. There would be time to dress up later. After five hours of getting breakfast served, helping with other people's clothes, supervising the erection of the tent in the backyard, making sure the indoor heaters were working properly, and directing the people who had come to set up chairs and tables and buffet tables, she went in to have lunch and make sure Frank didn't need any more help, and then finally went upstairs to dress. The life of an inn manager—but she wouldn't trade it for anything.

Arriving back downstairs, she flipped through a few pages on her clipboard and made final adjustments to things.

"Can you please make sure the cat is not hanging from the drapes inside when they take the wedding pictures?" Adele asked Joe, the college student who was helping out for the weekend. Several of the couples in the wedding were staying tonight also, to see the bride and groom for brunch in the morning. Everyone's kids were coming in this time and staying for the night also. The cat should have gone to Chelsea's mom's, but Zoe had said the cat could stay, and it was one less thing they had to do if it stayed.

Joe laughed and shrugged. "I'll try, Adele, but you know how fast and nosy that thing is."

119

Yes, she did. In the past almost three months the kitten had become a cat that ran around the house like a demon. It was adorable, but it added a new layer of responsibility to her duties. Fortunately, so far they had not had any real issues with the cat other than an insatiable curiosity about everything.

She brushed a hand across the newel post at the bottom of the stairs as she walked by on her way to the kitchen to make sure Frank was in his glory. He was catering the whole thing with the help of some culinary students from the local college. It was a new program Adele had started four months ago, and she was excited to see it come to fruition.

Stopping at the entrance to the living room, she looked in to make sure all the furniture was where it was supposed to be and no cat in sight. Good to go.

The last few months had been so hectic, with moving Chelsea to town from her previous residence and planning this wedding. And then Jack's sister had her baby, an adorable little boy they had all been eagerly anticipating.

She'd had a ton of help from Paige, Jack's sister, who was a real wedding planner. They'd talked about bringing her into the business, but Paige herself had nixed the idea because she wanted to be independent and to have time with her son. Instead they simply referred people to her and then paid her a fee when they had their own questions.

She'd be here today, and Adele would see if there was a moment when she could pull her aside to ask how the visitations the little boy's dad had demanded were going. Chelsea and Jack had now been out with Paige and her ex three times for dinner. Neutral territory, they said. But with Christmas in two weeks, he'd said he wanted an actual Christmas. It was something they were all working on making happen. Then again, today might not be the right day to ask about that. There was always tomorrow.

Opening the swinging door into the kitchen, Adele smiled when she found Mazzy standing on a kitchen chair helping Frank put the finishing touches on the gigantic salad bowls they'd put out in a few hours.

The cake had already been delivered from Decadence. Mazzy spotted her from her position in the doorway and squealed in glee.

Frank helped her down from the chair, making sure she was steady on her feet before letting her go to run at Adele's legs.

Adele had never considered herself a little woman in any sense of the word, but Mazzy was a pure ball of energy that could bowl over a sumo wrestler if given enough starting room.

She was ready, though, braced as she was against the wall next to the door. When Mazzy made contact, Adele lifted her into the air and gave her a smacking kiss on the cheek.

Mazzy wrapped her arms around her neck and nearly choked her in what should have been a hug.

"You get stronger every day!" Adele said.

"Is all the veggies Mr. Frank makes me eat!"

"Well, keep it up and you might be able to wrestle Mr. Frank." Adele giggled when Frank just rolled his eyes at her.

"Please don't go giving her any ideas. I'm still trying to recover from my sound beating at the ping-pong table Jack put in the back part of the basement."

That got a full-out laugh from both her and Mazzy. Mazzy had not played so much as aimed and hit Frank with ball after ball since he wasn't fast enough to get out of her path once she got started.

"Are we all ready in here?" she asked.

"Ready as we'll ever be." Frank covered the salad with cellophane and walked it to the enormous refrigerator in the back corner where everything else was stored for this big day.

"Good."

"Who helped you with the dishes last night? There's no way you'd look this chipper if you'd cleaned everything on your own."

Despite the blush creeping up her neck, Adele looked him dead in the eye. "Logan helped."

"Interesting." He smiled with mischief in his eyes. "His mom's told me a thing or two about him. I gotta say, I find it fascinating that he washed dishes with you. Did he do anything else with you?" Frank raised an eyebrow at her, and she willed him not to say anything more about Logan.

"Ah, no."

"No secret video games?"

She was caught. Clearing her throat, she stuck a fist on her hip. "Yes, we played a few rounds, but that was it, and then he went home."

"Shame, that. I like that boy, and you should too."

"I do like… Look, we have a wedding today. Let's keep our eyes on the prize at the end of the day."

Frank snickered. "Aye, aye, captain," he said with a mock salute.

She stuck her tongue out at him, and Mazzy followed suit. Uh-oh. "Why don't you go help Mr.

Frank again, so I can do the rest of my last-minute checks?" she asked the precocious child, setting her down. Mazzy ran right back to Frank and gave him a huge hug as he put her back on her chair.

The older man had always been a gruff, stereotypical ex-service guy. That had changed since Mazzy came into the picture. He'd softened considerably. Not that she'd ever tell him that, since he'd probably bristle at her, but it was true. He was a huge softy now, when it came to that little girl.

Leaving them to their work, Adele walked back through the sitting room and the library. Everything was in place, even if her mind wasn't completely following suit. Would Logan show up with someone? Was she being stupid to think he might be interested in her? Or did he just see her as one of the guys? It wouldn't be the first time…

****

This monkey suit was not his thing. Logan gladly would have foregone this wedding if it weren't for Dex and Zoe. Hell, he'd been to more weddings in the past few months than in his whole freaking life. Logan was more of a jeans and T-shirts kind of guy. Not this tux thing that he'd had to cram himself into. He'd even go with a suit and tie, sure, but this was going to be a sunset wedding and the invitation specifically said formal attire. Which meant the monkey suit.

Standing in front of his bathroom mirror, he tried again to get the damn bowtie tied. It had come with instructions. He wished it had come with a clip instead. That he could do, but tying the thing was becoming the bane of his existence.

He tried one more time, and the thing looked at

least halfway decent. It would have to do.

He ran a comb through his short hair, checked to make sure his teeth and nails were clean, and then called himself done.

He was not going to be the main attraction at this thing, so as long as he looked marginally fine, he was good.

Stepping out the front door, he waved to his neighbor across the hallway as she exited her own apartment.

"Well, hey, there. Where are you off to, cutie?" she asked, the load of laundry under her arm cocked on her hip.

"Wedding." He turned and made sure his apartment door was locked, then flipped her a wave as he headed down the stairs.

"I hope you catch the garter," she called after him.

Yeah, that was the last thing he wanted to do.

Cars were everywhere when he pulled up at the inn. A certain woman with flaming red hair and curves galore came to mind, but she'd be busy, and it would be better if he didn't try to hunt her down even if he could get it together enough to ask her out. She was all he had thought about last night in his big bed, all by himself. How soft her skin would be, what it would be like to have her next to him. Under him. Over him. That glorious hair out of its ponytail and cascading around them to make a curtain. The fact that she was funny, interesting, and great to hang with entered into the equation, too, and it set him on edge.

Leaving his car in the grass, he walked around the addition he and Nate had recently put on the house. It had been tough to get it done on time. He patted the side of the house as he rounded the corner and came into the back garden. A huge tent took up most of the backyard. Fortunately, they hadn't yet had snow. He'd heard that a big storm was on its way for Christmas. As long as today stayed clear, though, it would be good.

People were milling around in the near-forty-degree weather, so at least he had made it on time. He looked around for Nate, to see if Claudia could fix his bowtie properly.

Instead Adele found him, the woman with the flaming red hair, who had starred in his every dream last night.

"Oh, that's not going to do, Logan. Let me fix you."

And she went to work on his tie with nimble fingers. He couldn't help but breathe in the light lilac smell wafting off her. He'd interacted with her a lot over the last several weeks as the project went from idea to completion. She was pretty in a fiery way, her red hair stacked on top of her head in what looked like a messy bun but had probably taken hours to perfect. Her bangs swung to the side, highlighting her pretty blue eyes.

The first time he'd seen her, he'd been in professional mode. Now? Well, now he admitted he was interested, very interested. And now that they knew each other better and she'd beat him at his favorite pastime, he was smitten. But he just wasn't sure if she felt the same.

He stood still while she fixed his tie, her eyes concentrated on his neck. He tried not to swallow and make his Adam's apple bob, but it was a tough thing. Up this close, he realized that though she seemed taller, she really only came to his shoulder, in her blue heels, and she had to look up to work on his tie.

She caught him looking at her, as she finished up with retying the piece of cloth, and smiled at him. Patting his neck and chest with her palm, she said, "There you go, all done. I hope you have a good time tonight."

He cleared his throat. "Thanks, you too."

And she walked away, calling out to someone named Joe and telling him to make sure the cat stayed in the back bedroom. He watched the swish of the bottom of her dress where it hit her mid-calf, his eyes then traveling up to her rounded backside, to her waist, and farther to her back and her shoulders, where a silver-and-blue shawl-like thing draped over her arms and down her back. With her hair swept up, the back of her neck looked good enough to nibble on, right there where fine red hairs rioted in curls that he'd bet were soft to the touch.

Nate elbowed him from the left, jolting him clear out of his case of lust. Thank God, too. He had the jacket of the monkey suit buttoned, but he wasn't sure it would completely hide his growing erection. Not exactly how he wanted to walk around for the wedding. Reciting some of the button combinations for the video games he liked to play in his downtime, he willed his cock to deflate asap.

It worked, and so did the second elbow he got from his slightly older brother.

"So, Logan, you got your eye out for any girl in particular tonight, or are you just waiting to see who has the worst wedding fever?"

"You're lucky Claudia isn't next to you or she

would kick your ass for saying that."

Nate chuckled. "True, but that doesn't answer my question. You haven't dated anyone new in weeks, and that's just not like you. So have you picked someone out, or are you going with the flow? Or have you finally said something to Miss Inn Runner?"

Logan shrugged. He was not going to tell Nate that the reason he hadn't started anything new recently was because he couldn't seem to get the red hair and blue eyes of his current check signer out of his head. Fraternizing with the client was frowned upon, but this was different, and he knew it. His dad liked her, Claudia and Nate liked her. Hell, all of his family and friends liked her. Would he mess it up? Did she care at all? He wasn't sure, and that still made him hesitate. But he was tempted. Man, was he tempted.

"Nah, I'm just here long enough to give my good wishes, and then I'm headed home to get out of this tux."

"Well, we'd better get you a chair. The wedding's about to start. And don't forget you have to stay for the dance."

"Right." Logan followed Nate to the second row, where white plastic chairs were situated in the tent and tied with deep blue ribbons on the back. Silver and blue flowers filled a trellis. A minister stood under the trellis, and four men stood up front. Nate made a dash to stand at the end, filling out the groomsmen, while Logan grabbed a chair.

He was in the dance, but he wasn't a groomsman. That was fine with him, since he didn't think Zoe would be happy with unbalanced numbers.

He hadn't been able to resist the request to join in

the dance, though. Maybe he could grab Adele as his partner…

Chapter Five

The music swelled as the bridesmaids each took their stroll down the aisle. Zoe had wanted them to alternately wear blue and silver and had found beautiful flowing dresses in soft velvet that flattered each of the body types present in the wedding party. She'd asked Adele to be one of her attendants, but Adele had known she was better suited to being behind the scenes. She had left most of the planning up to Paige, while Adele made sure the staging and procession went down the right way.

She shifted from foot to foot as the vows were said, then walked to the rear of the tent they'd had set up in the garden to cover the dance floor. It was surrounded by ten round tables covered with alternating blue and silver tablecloths. The centerpieces had turned out beautifully, with snowflakes and keepsake Christmas decorations in the form of glass balls with Zoe and Dex's wedding date etched into them. They'd spent hours making all the name place tags and sticking them in silver card holders that another friend of Jack's had made. Sam Locke was a talented metalworker, and they'd hooked him up with Paige to do custom work as needed.

Everything was ready, and not a moment too soon as the bride and groom came through a human arch of their friends and family holding hands over their heads.

Adele smiled, then got down to business trying to get everyone situated in their correct places so dinner could be served, the cake cut, dances danced, and the happy couple enjoyed before they went off to their room, which she had spruced up this morning with candles and rose petals at Dex's request.

Things sped by after that. Once dinner was served, Zoe and Dex went to take a few pictures. They'd been adamant about not having a three-hour lag to take photos that, yes, they'd cherish but not as much as making memories with their friends and family.

The DJ kicked up the music, encouraging people to dance, and Adele stood at the back of the tent, ready for any emergency or need. This was her calling, and she was so lucky that Jack had hired her young and given her the chance to shine in something she did well. She'd gone to school for hotel management despite a few setbacks, and Jack had hired her straight out of college. They hadn't done many weddings before now, their guests being mostly people up to look at the fall flowers or doing family reunions, or those just looking to get away. But Chelsea changed all that when she came here to help with her sister's wedding.

It hadn't gone exactly as they thought it would, but it had opened the door for others to call and ask for their services. And this wedding was a long time coming and therefore quite a happy one to celebrate. She wanted it to be perfect, and it was so far. She hadn't even seen the cat in at least an hour.

Once the cake was cut and Adele brought out more plates because they had underestimated the number of people who wanted both the chocolate and the swirl but not on the same plate, it was time for the dancing to begin in earnest.

She fought back tears as Dex and Zoe shared their first dance and then danced with her parents. Dex's brother then came to get Zoe, and Delly, Dex's sister-in-law, came for him, since Dex's parents had died years ago.

And then it was the money dance, which she provided the pouches for, silently handing them over and then fading into the background again.

After that dance, the room got quiet. She had no idea what was happening when the lights were turned down, only leaving the twinkling lights at the apex of the roof. This was not scheduled. A popular song about marrying blasted out from the DJ station, and then Nate, Dex, Sam, Jack, and Logan were spotlighted in the middle of the dance floor.

Hooting and hollering followed when Jocelyn brought a stunned Zoe forward and made her stand at the edge of the dance floor. Dex came sliding across the floor in his tux pants and thrust his hand out to her. He rose to his feet and sang to her as he backed away and joined the guys behind him in what was quite honestly a pretty impressive dance. There weren't many moves, but they'd combined them in ways that made it clear Jocelyn must have had a hand in the performance. Zoe was laughing, as were many others, and everyone clapped in time with the music.

The song changed, and each of the guys came out into the audience and grabbed their significant other. Everyone that is, except Logan. He made eye contact with her and raised an eyebrow. She looked over her shoulder because he couldn't really be looking at her.

But yes, he was.

She tried to look busy doing something, anything, but there was nothing to do. And then she was caught up in his strong arms and whirled onto the dance floor.

"I hope you don't mind that I didn't formally ask you." He brought her close, and she would have sworn he sniffed her, but that was ridiculous to even think.

"No, that's, um, okay." Maintaining distance with this big man was not going to happen, though she tried. For every inch she moved back, he reeled her in two, until finally she gave up and just sank into his arms. With one hand on her back, he folded his other hand around hers and led her in a waltz. She knew the steps from watching Cinderella with Mazzy and had no trouble understanding how a woman could be caught up when dancing with a dashing man. He led her around the floor with a grace she didn't know he had. Yet another facet of this man that she couldn't quite fit into the puzzle.

But, oh, how she wanted to put it together.

Even with the guy who had written her the letter she hadn't wanted to know as much about him, spend more time with him, or know everything about him. Not really.

If she were honest with herself—and maybe now wasn't the best time, but she wasn't going to hide from it—she had to admit that it was truly just an affair, not meant to last longer than it had. He'd done her a favor by walking away. He could have been nicer about it, could have written sooner or said goodbye. But in the end, it all led her to being in Logan's arms, and she couldn't regret that.

It might not last more than a few days, they might just end up friends, but at this moment she wanted to find out. She hadn't wanted to find out about someone in years, even before the writer.

Then the dance was over. He led her back to her spot next to the DJ, kissed her knuckles, and went to finish in a grand finale with the guys in front of Zoe.

This might not have been on her schedule of events for the wedding, but she wouldn't have missed it for anything.

Then it was back to business as everyone talked and laughed and congratulated the guys and Jocelyn on the dance.

She called Joe out with a chair, and it was time for the throwing of the bouquet and the garter. Garter first. Dex gave Zoe a smile that would have lit up the earth by itself as the sun dipped below the mountains and the fairy lights strung along the inside of the tent flared to life. He took his time, and Zoe blushed at the intensity of the moment as he snaked his hand up under her dress. Her breath caught when he kissed Zoe on her knee.

Adele's breath caught, too, along with that of probably every other woman in the room. The guys wolf-whistled.

Someday. She'd always thought someday she would have someone who looked at her like that, touched her like that, but no one had come along, and with her job, she rarely got out. And now there might be hope, if Logan wasn't just looking for his next arm candy.

And if he was? She asked herself the hard question. If he was, then she would enjoy it while it lasted, consider it a rebound, and maybe think about getting back out there to see if anyone else caught her interest.

She was a free woman, had a great job, and would have more time now to be outside the inn. Maybe it really was time to let the past go and move into the future. She could be arm candy if she had to be, or maybe he would be her arm candy for a little while. Who knew?

Shaking the thoughts off, she laughed with everyone else when Dex threatened to duck under the beautiful lace-and-satin dress May at Decadence had outdone herself on. Zoe threatened to just take the darned thing off herself, and then he made quick work of the rest of it.

He turned around and shot the garter over his head. There were more single guys than she would have anticipated lined up waiting for the garter to bounce off the ceiling of the tent and fall into their waiting hands. It might have had something to do with knowing that once the bouquet was caught, they would get to put the garter on the flower catcher. She'd been to a wedding or two, and sometimes they turned into very randy affairs right after it was all said and done.

Next up, Zoe turned her back to the crowd and called all the ladies.

Jack snuck up next to Adele without her realizing it. "Go on out there. You're a single lady."

She laughed. "Yeah, no thanks. I have plenty to do without being the next to get married. Is Paige around? Maybe she should be out there."

"My sister's not going to want to catch a bouquet just yet, honey. Plus, I don't know if I want Logan putting a garter on her."

"Oh, is that who caught the garter?" She told her heart to cease its fluttering.

"Yep, so you can get out there."

"No, that's okay…Jaaaaack!" she yelled as she was thrust into the crowd of ladies from the back. She turned to glare at him, throwing her hands up in the air, and was about to stalk back to him when something brushed her hand. She closed her hand without thinking, and her stomach lurched when she realized she had grabbed the bouquet out of the air.

Well, she thought on a hitching breath, this ought to be interesting. There was a collective groan from the other women waiting to catch the bouquet.

"I'll get you for this," she mouthed to the laughing Jack. Chelsea came to kiss her on the cheek as she led her over to the chair where Zoe had previously sat for the kiss and de-gartering that had made Adele's heart flutter.

She'd fixed the guy's bow tie earlier. Surely she could appeal to him to just make it quick and done. They'd played video games together and eaten pizza. There was no need to go all out with the sexy music and the tease and games. She'd just ask him to be quick, so she could get back to her job in the background.

But when she had been set on the chair, Logan stalked around the rented floor, twirling the garter around his finger with a smirk on his face. This was not going to go well. She could feel it in her newly clutched gut.

Maybe she wasn't as ready as she thought. Or maybe she just didn't want it to be quite so public the first time she let a guy touch her leg in forever.

Now, though, he was coming toward her, with a smile that she could only describe as brilliant. His white teeth flashed in his tanned face. A dimple popped out in his left cheek when he waggled his eyebrows at her. He sauntered to the 1920s burlesque music like he was made for the stuff.

That fluttering-heart thing went into overdrive, and she very sternly gave herself a lecture to calm the hell down. It was all for show. She'd been to weddings before, and even if the two people forced to do this ritual hated each other, they still played their parts to get the crowd going and keep the atmosphere of fun and celebration running high. This was nothing more than that.

Sitting in the chair, she arranged her dark blue calf-length dress around her as best she could so he wouldn't have to get too handsy when putting the garter on her. She'd whisper to him, if she had to, that the knee was a fine place to stop, and then they could all laugh with the crowd.

He bent his knee and knelt before her, his shiny black shoes catching the glow from the twinkling lights above. Those teeth flashed again; he was enjoying this way too much. Most likely he was a show-off, and this was his element.

With those good looks, he'd probably made every girl in this room swoon at one time or another. She tried to remember that and kept telling it to herself as he lifted her foot, slipped her shoe off, and rested her stockinged toes on his thigh. The warmth of him through his black tux pants made her toes curl. That was all it was, just the warmth.

"Can we please keep this quick and clean?" she whispered through barely moving lips.

"I doubt it. And, my dear Adele, even if I could, I don't think I want to."

Oh, no.

Chapter Six

She wore nylons. Of course Logan was aware they made them, but so few women wore them. Certainly the ones he had dated recently hated them and didn't wear them. The silky slide of his fingers over her leg made him instantly rock hard. He hadn't had this kind of reaction since he was a randy teenager.

A brief vision flashed in his mind of him as a little boy. There was a picture at Halloween of him standing between his mom and his aunt, who had both dressed up as flappers. They'd had stockings on, and his mom liked to tell the story where he just kept running his hands up and down their calves because he liked the texture, even at that young age. Apparently that like had turned into a little something more, when it involved this particular woman and these particular nylons.

He was not going to rush this, and the catcalls from the audience only egged him on.

Creeping the garter up her leg one inch at a time, he rocked it back and forth. Someone called out for him to take it all the way up, and he smiled. It wasn't as if that thought hadn't entered his mind already. But she had asked for clean. He could give her that, even if he had no intention of giving her the quick part.

Her full cheeks blossomed with an enticing blush when he got to her calf and inched his way under her skirt. Would it be pressing his luck to go just a little bit further? Would he ever get this chance again?

She certainly wasn't ignoring him now as she alternated between looking into his eyes and looking back down at the progress of the garter.

He decided that just above the knee would probably both satisfy her desire and not spike his too high.

However, when he passed over the bend in her knee, she whispered, "Please," and he took it just two inches more. Where he encountered warm bare flesh and the edge of a stocking, he nearly went off like a rocket. She wasn't just wearing nylons—she was wearing thigh-highs.

"Go out with me just once, and I'll stop," he said low enough for only her ears.

She stared at him with wide eyes. "What?" she whispered back.

"One date, and I'll stop." He threw in what he hoped was his best smile and prayed it didn't look desperate.

Those wide eyes were still staring. He sent the garter another quarter of an inch north, letting his fingers rest on the skin of her smooth thigh.

"Fine," she said. And either it was said breathlessly or in another whisper. He'd prefer the former but would gladly take the latter, since it was the answer he wanted. "But this is coercion," she added.

He laughed, long and loud and bent forward to kiss her square on the mouth. More catcalls and whistles and a few gasps later, he released her soft lips.

Looking her square in the eye, he smiled. "I call it meant."

She inhaled sharply, and two tiny lines appeared

between her perfect auburn eyebrows. He stepped back from her to do an exaggerated bow to the clapping and cat-calling going on in the big tent. Nate gave him a quizzical look, but Logan ignored it in favor of taking Adele's hand to assist in lifting her from the chair. Traditionally this was where he shared a dance with her. He wasn't letting her get away. After feeling the skin of her thigh, and dancing with her before, he wanted her in his arms again.

The music changed from 1920s bawdy house teaser music to a slow dance. With desire swirling around inside him, he captured her in his arms. Wrapping her tight, he waited an agonizing ten seconds for her to relax enough to put her arms around his neck and not stand still like a mannequin.

Once she unbent a little, he could feel every curve and dip in her luscious body. Resolutely, he thought of every tool in his toolbox, one by one, and then all of the stock they had at the warehouse at the back of the business, each category, every stack, to keep himself from getting hard again.

Of course that was a lot of thinking about wood and steel, which didn't exactly help in the least. It was the best he could do, however.

"Are you enjoying the wedding?" he asked in an effort to distract himself further. He'd just gotten a whiff of the curve of her neck, and she still smelled like lilacs, one of his favorite fragrances.

"Yes, but you're bad," she said, arching back out of contact so that her breasts just grazed his chest instead of being pressed into him. That was more torture than having her in full body contact. He couldn't believe that was possible. The proof was evident in the way his heart thundered inside his chest.

"What's that supposed to mean?"

She frowned at him. "You know what it means. You could have stopped, but no."

"Did you really want me to stop?" he asked. That pounding heart nearly stopped when she smiled coyly.

"I think if I was going to have your hands on me, I would have preferred a place a little more private." She blushed, making him want to kiss the top of her rounded cheeks, just there under her left eye where a small crinkle formed.

"People expect a show at weddings. And I really wanted to get my hands on you again."

"Are you toying with me? Do you really want to go out on a date, or is this just some kind of pity thing?"

She couldn't be that dense. "No toying. I have been trying to get the guts together to ask you for weeks, and the opportunity presented itself. If you really don't want to go, you don't have to. I've never had to blackmail anyone into dating me before." He smiled again, but her frown didn't lessen. He was not going about this the right way, and he knew it. The problem was he didn't know how to fix it.

"I'm having a hard time believing you had to get up courage to ask me out."

"Then you underestimate yourself—and my intentions," he said with all the sincerity he felt.

The frown disappeared, and the lines between her eyebrows smoothed out. "Touché."

It wasn't exactly a yes. He wasn't going to challenge it, though, since he'd already gotten one of those out of her tonight. Pressing his luck for another would be a mistake. That could come tomorrow night, when he took her to dinner.

****

What had she been thinking? Adele stood in front of her closet on the third floor of the inn, trying to think about the impression she wanted to make at dinner tonight. Truthfully, she wanted to make no impression at all. Although if she was going to lie to herself that she was being truthful, she really should have a nose about a yard long.

There was a part of her which had liquefied and sighed as she'd danced with Logan last night at Dex's wedding. He had been smooth, and after she'd given him his due for pointing out how she might just be underestimating herself and his interest, they'd talked about inconsequential things and how happy they were that his brother and her friend were married. No more sparring, no more smiles aimed at her. And she'd told herself that was fine, but was it really?

She had to refocus on the closet. Logan was going to be here in twenty minutes, yet she still hadn't picked something out of the big closet of dresses, pants, and shirts. The one thing she'd asked Jack to approve for the remodel was a walk-in closet put in her room. He'd more than agreed, even taken it a step further and had his old room that was between hers and Frank's turned into a sitting room for just her. Frank got to keep the living room with its flashing beer signs and recliners. Her sitting room got the jukebox from the living room and as many bookshelves as they could fit. Yes, there was a perfectly good library downstairs, but after five years she wanted a place that was her own. Now had seemed like the perfect time to ask for it.

Fortunately, Jack was so in love that she could

have asked for nearly anything to keep things on an even keel here at the inn.

Pulling out two blouses, Adele held each up in front of her chest to see which one she liked better. The answer was…neither, so she went back to looking and pawing through her extensive collection. She wanted something she didn't normally wear around the inn. She hadn't been out on a date in about five years. That gave her pause. Five whole years. Even when she'd had that brief affair with the guest at the inn, they had never gone anywhere but his room.

A sigh escaped her before she could stop it. Even now this would only be a one-time thing. There were no guarantees that when it was just them, with no games to distract or large crowds to fill in the silences, they would have anything to talk about.

She continued to stand in front of her closet, crossing one foot over the other, then shifting and recrossing them.

Throwing her hands into the air, she muffled a frustrated shriek. Hell, it didn't matter what she wore. He might have jokingly called it "meant" for them to both catch the things being thrown, but he probably didn't mean it. He was a playboy. She'd seen him many times around the small town of Kissinger. And he was always with a different girl. Long hair, short hair, tall or short, they were all thin and beautiful.

As she looked at herself in the mirror across the room on the back of her bedroom door, she sucked in her gut and thrust out her chest. She had long hair, and she was short, but she was a far cry from thin…

He probably didn't really want her "that way" anyway.

With that in mind, she grabbed a teal-colored mid-calf dress, plopped it over her head, whipped her hair into a messy but still pretty bun, swiped on some eyeliner and mascara, and called herself done about thirty seconds before Logan rang the doorbell.

She was halfway down the last staircase to the front door when she saw him in the sidelights framing the front door. He really was handsome. From the hair that hung just over his collar to the way his blue eyes creased at the corners when he was laughing, he was the total package. And she had no idea why he would want to go out with her.

She stepped back as she opened the door with a forced smile. This was a bad idea. She'd fake it, though. A couple hours was not going to kill her. "Hey, right on time. I like punctuality," she said, trying to think of him as a guest, or a prospective guest, or maybe even a businessman who was taking her to dinner to discuss a new brand of linens to carry at the inn.

"Wow. You look great!" he said, the flowers in his hands tipping over to the side.

She saved them by cupping his hand before he dropped them, and she laughed. "You sound surprised. Thanks, I think."

"No not surprised, more like astounded. I thought you looked great last night. Tonight you look even better."

There would be no preening, she told herself very sternly. Her whole thing about him probably not wanting to take her out again still firmly in her mind, she thanked him and let it go.

"Did you want to come in for a minute?" she asked, holding the door open behind her.

"Sure. You might want to grab a jacket for where we're going. It could get a little chilly."

Where on earth were they going? But she wasn't going to ask, because that felt predictable. If she wasn't going to be asked out again for another five years, she wanted this to be a night she remembered.

Chapter Seven

Logan tried hard, he really did, to keep his eyes on the road, but the way her red hair was piled on top of her head, and the light makeup along with that lilac scent filling the cab of his truck hit him in a way he couldn't resist.

He had to impress her tonight. As far as he knew, she'd never gone out with anyone in town. He'd even asked Nate if he knew of anyone she'd ever dated, and both he and his wife Claudia had drawn a blank.

She was so busy at the inn lately that maybe she chose not to date, and here he had coerced her into this. But coercion or not, dating outside of town or not, he was not going to make this just one more date in a long line of dates. There was something about Adele that made him want to be better and really put effort into this.

So he'd called his cousin, Benny, and asked if there was a dinner tonight. Sure enough, there was, and he really hoped the crowd was a good one.

Pulling into the parking lot of the small island in the middle of the river that ran past the capitol of Pennsylvania, he watched her look around as if she wasn't quite sure where they were.

He laid an arm over the back of the cab seat, turning his body toward her. "Have you ever been on the Susquehanna?"

"Um, no." She gave her head a little shake, and his gut clenched. He hadn't even thought to ask if she got seasick. Christ Almighty, could he have been any dumber?

"You don't get seasick, do you?"

She laughed, a sound he enjoyed and one he'd heard throughout the house over the last few weeks. Now, it hit him low in the gut, when before it just made him smile. He had it bad.

"No, I don't get seasick, and I'd hardly call a river that's normally less than four feet deep anything like the sea."

"Right." Now he felt stupid.

"But I appreciate your asking."

Well, at least he didn't feel as stupid.

"Are we going on a pontoon or something? You do realize it's winter, even if the temperatures have been higher than normal." She peered through the windshield, oblivious to how close his hand was to her semi-exposed back. He'd walked behind her when they were heading to his truck, and the back of the dress was actually better than the front, though he would have been hard pressed to guess that right if he'd been asked.

"Or something."

She waited a beat. "Are you going to tell me what that something is?"

"Do you want to know, or do you like surprises?"

She peered at him as she took another moment. He could almost see the gears turning in her head.

"I can stand a surprise here or there, but normally I like to go in with both eyes open."

"Fair enough. We're going on a twilight cruise on the old steamboat."

Her blue eyes widened as she clasped her hands in front of her chest. "Really? I thought you had to buy tickets way in advance for that." Excitement radiated in her voice. "I've tried getting guests on for one of their whim trips, and I've never been able to snag tickets."

He smiled. "Sometimes it's all about who you know."

He liked that she waited as he got out of the truck to come around to open her door. He'd never completely understood women who were against men acting like gentlemen. He was fully aware that Adele could have opened the door by herself and gotten out of the truck herself. Hell, she could have driven it just as well as he did, but he liked some of the older manners. It was rough when you ended up with someone who would fight you for the door just to prove they didn't need you.

Helping her out of the passenger's side allowed him to slide a hand from her shoulder to her wrist. She was as soft here as her thigh had been. It made him crave in a way he never had before. Down, boy, he told himself.

She thanked him when her feet hit the ground, then moved out of the way while he closed the door. He crooked his arm at the elbow to escort her along the gravel path, and she took it.

Strolling along, they talked about little, but it wasn't awkward. She would look around and point things out to him, like a mourning dove on a low branch or a puppy running around off its leash on the small beach on the side of the island.

And then they were at the steamboat, where he got a little nervous. What if she didn't like the music or the dinner? At this point he couldn't turn back, but he'd never taken anyone to one of these. Truthfully, he wasn't sure why he had decided to do this now. His love of swing music wasn't exactly a secret, but it wasn't something most people under eighty really shared. He was a hit at the nursing homes when he was there doing repairs because he always had the CD player stacked with big band music. The oldsters would get up and shake a leg or two, then laugh and sit back down.

Here, though, it was going to be a real big band night. He hoped she was not more into classical or contemporary. Or one of those people who hated anything without a synthesizer attached to it.

Well, he was here now. Even if she hated it, at least that would be an answer in itself for him. He was tired of wasting his time with women who didn't get him and didn't want to get him other than for his prowess in bed or the good money he made working for his dad. He finally wanted something real and lasting, and this was a big part of him.

"You're awfully quiet all of a sudden," she said, tugging a little bit on his arm.

"Just thinking."

"About what?"

The music was low key as they went up the gangplank to the paddleboat. It was dressed in ragtime, and the music reflected the era. He watched her for signs of disgust or boredom, but her eyes actually seemed to light up, and she held onto his arm a little tighter. When she gave a little wiggle, he grinned.

"You like the music?"

She nodded with a big smile on her face.

"Do you listen to this kind of music, or is this one of those things where it brings back great memories of your grandparents?"

She laughed and shook her head.

"Have you lost the ability to speak?"

Now she laughed even harder as they stepped up into the boat itself and the music swelled.

He was about to ask her if she was laughing at him instead of in joy when she kicked up a heel with each step. He was pretty sure that thump was the sound of him falling instantly in love.

****

Had he asked Frank, or had Jack said something to Logan? She knew they sometimes made fun of her for her love of swing music, but she didn't think they would have put Logan up to this. When would they have had time? She knew they harped on her constantly to get a life, yet this was a little too much.

However, she was not going to look a night on a steamboat with swing music in the face and ignore it. She would have to calm her desire to dance, though. Logan had been good out on the dance floor at Dex's wedding, but this was a whole other level of dancing.

"I love this music for both reasons," she answered him, trying hard not to sound breathy. It was hard because it felt like her entire being had lit up, from her toes to her nose. She loved the big band era, with the outfits and the style and the time period itself. Sure there had been bad things going on, no era existed without them, but there was such happiness, such brightness in a time when things were going to hell during that time in history, and some of the best music ever had been produced.

She nearly dragged Logan on deck in search of where the music was coming from. If it was live, she wasn't sure she was going to be able to contain herself.

"Slow down a second." He grinned at her. "I have to check in for our reservations, and I've arranged a few things. Do you mind standing right here for a few minutes? I'll be right back."

She could stand here forever. "Sure." She clutched her purse against her belly and smiled at the few people who walked by. She should have brought business cards, just in case she got into talks with any of the tourists. Normally she thought of things like that. Tonight she had been nervous and she'd forgotten.

That was so unlike her. Although it wasn't a bad thing, necessarily. Maybe it was time for her to unbend a little.

Logan walked back to her. He had a decidedly masculine walk, with his arms swinging and his strides big. He'd shortened them to accommodate her when they came from the parking lot.

She'd appreciated that. She appreciated not having to run to catch up with him, either.

Behind him he had a big guy, tall and wide. The grin on the man's face nearly split his cheeks in two.

"Hello, pretty lady."

She knew he was talking to her since she was the only one on this particular spot on the boat, but she had to keep herself from checking over her shoulder. Instead she put her best smile on and held her hand out to shake when he was close enough. Instead, he pulled her into a bear hug so big she almost lost her balance.

He set her back on her feet a moment later, then stepped back, keeping her hands in his. "So Logan brought a lady friend."

"I don't know that we're friends yet," she said, causing a blush to run rampant over her skin. Nice way to cram her foot in her mouth before they even got started.

But Logan laughed. "I'll have her changing her tune by the end of the night."

"No doubt in my mind, my man." He squeezed Logan's shoulder and gave her a wink. "Harry Borden, at your service, little lady. You need anything, you just ask for Harry, and I'll fix it. Even if this boy here gets fresh." Another wink and he walked away.

What followed was a night of music, laughter, some dancing by the two of them, and some marvelous dancing to watch as other couples got up and did the big dances. Flushed, Adele sat down after their last jitterbug, laughing and smiling.

"That was awesome!"

"I'm not as good as those guys out there, but I have fun." Logan motioned for drinks, and a water pitcher was brought to the table with lemon slices floating in it.

"This is fun." She waited while he poured her a glass.

"It is. I've never brought anyone here before."

That almost sounded like a confession, and she didn't know what to say back. "Thank you."

"Thanks for being open to the experience. Would you be willing to come again in the spring? This is the last cruise before they pull the boat out for repairs over the winter."

She could be cautious or she could go for it. She went for it. "Would that be our second date, then? Three months from now?"

He peered at her across the table with the candlelight flickering in the small cut crystal votive holder. "I guess that depends on you."

"How so?" She gripped her hands tightly in her lap.

"Well, I'll be honest if you will." His long fingers tapped on the tabletop in a syncopated rhythm that did not match the tune the band was playing. Was he as nervous as she was?

Nodding her head, she encouraged him to say whatever he had on his mind first. She would be as honest as she could be, depending on what he said.

More tapping. He looked down at his fingers, then stilled his hand. Looking into her eyes, he opened his palm out on the white linen, his fingers slightly curled.

She put her hand in his, feeling a jolt that had nothing to do with electricity but everything to do with a connection.

"I know you think I take a new girl out all the time, and you're not wrong. But I want something more with you, Adele. We have a lot to learn about each other. I know that. I'm not expecting to move right past the dating stage and into a long-term relationship immediately, but if I'm being honest, then I'd like this to be the first of many dates. I know what it's like to enjoy being with someone but not feel that extra something that makes you want to hang around for the ups and the downs." He caressed the inside of her wrist. "I know what it's like to give up because it just doesn't seem like there's enough there to put the effort into making a real relationship. But I want to make the effort with you. I want to hang around, and I want to be here for as many dates as you'll have me for."

Honesty could be a beautiful thing. She had enough of her own to give back. "You're the first man I've actually dated since high school, Logan. My last foray into this territory ended up being a disaster that hung over my head for years. But I want what you want. You make me laugh, you make me smile, and you make me think. I want that, and I'll want dates with you for the long term." She didn't say forever. That might be too much too fast. But it was what she was thinking.

And it was what she tasted on his lips when he pulled her around the table into his lap and kissed her with his hands cradling her face.

"I think I love you," he murmured against her lips.

"Let's see if I can't change your tune to drop that 'I think,' " she whispered in his ear as she nipped his lobe.

"I'm willing to be coerced. More than willing."

She was pretty sure it wasn't going to take a lot to convince him, but she was willing to give it her all—no regrets, no rebounds, no doubts. Just all of her and all of him, and together they'd figured it out as they went along. She couldn't ask for more than that.

"You're looking serious," he said, kissing her knuckles again.

"Seriously contemplating if I can sneak you into the inn without anyone noticing."

He kissed her, then laughed. "I have every confidence in you."

And that made all the difference.

Maybe
This Time

by

Misty Simon

Misty Simon

Chapter One

Locking the door behind her, Paige Barton lugged the baby carrier, the diaper bag, and her own purse to the car. The forecast called for snow tonight, so she had packed extra for both herself and Ian for a couple of days in case she didn't feel like coming back to her apartment right after Christmas.

Her brother and sister-in-law had tried to talk her into staying over through the holidays to the New Year. They had plenty of room at that huge inn they owned on the outskirts of Kissinger, but she wasn't sure if she would feel up to socializing that much, after this latest setback with her ex, the father of her baby. She might be in desperate need of an out, to hole herself back up in her apartment if necessary.

Last night she was supposed to have met her ex-boyfriend, Mason Nottingham, in a place other than a restaurant for the first time since Ian was born. He'd contacted her two months ago to see their child, and she'd ignored him. Or she'd tried to, until he subtly hinted that he'd go after custody if she didn't play nice. In the first place, he didn't deserve anything from her or to see Ian. He had walked, without a word, when Paige was only three months pregnant.

The pregnancy had come as a shock to her as much as to him. She'd expected there to be issues, since they had only been seeing each other for about five months and hadn't made any kind of real commitment, but his stuttering over it had made her feel about two inches tall.

She had made peace with the situation fairly quickly, but he had simply stared at her while stuttering and then told her he needed time to think. A month went by, and she didn't bother him. After those thirty days, she wrote him off and hadn't looked back. He'd tried to contact her after that, but she'd ignored him.

So it was not exactly her idea to see him now. At this point, the only reason she had agreed to let him see Ian was because her friend Zoe's husband Dex was a lawyer and had told her it might be best to see what Mason wanted and try to settle outside of court instead of dragging things through the legal system. Mason had more money behind him than Paige did as an independent wedding consultant. She was pretty sure she wouldn't lose Ian, but she wasn't willing to risk it.

Mason had blown it, though, when he hadn't shown or called or even texted yesterday after completely missing their "Christmas" that he'd said he so desperately wanted.

And now it was Christmas Eve, and she was going to enjoy herself with all her friends and family and forget Mason's name. He could try again, and she might answer the phone, but she was angry, because she'd been ready to trust him again, her feelings resurfacing over those dinners where she'd used her brother and sister-in-law as a buffer. But the truth remained that she still loved the jerk and had wanted Ian to have the family he deserved—if only Mason had stepped up and kept his end of the bargain.

But he hadn't. Again.

Tucking Ian into the back seat of the car, she shut the door and opened the passenger side to deposit their bags. The trunk was already stuffed with presents, the playpen, and toys.

She believed in being prepared.

The drive across the river and through the back hills of Central Pennsylvania didn't take more than twenty minutes, but it felt like she was in a whole different world when tall buildings gave way to fields and farms and tiny towns with one main street. Driving through Kissinger, she waved to Claudia, May, and Zoe as they stood outside their shop, Decadence, to admire a new front window display they'd put in. Ever since her sister-in-law Chelsea had hooked Paige up with them, through working at the inn, her business had been booming. They made the cakes, the dresses, and the flowers, and she organized the whole thing. It worked out for all of them nicely. And it still allowed her to care for Ian all on her own.

It wasn't how she would have chosen to raise her son, but it was what she was left with. Claudia and Chelsea had both been godsends, telling her all about raising their own children alone and demanding she lean on them as well as her other friends that she thought of as sisters. She didn't know what she would have done without them, and she never wanted to find out.

She was strong, dammit, she told herself as she listened to Ian coo in the back seat. She checked him in the rearview mirror and found him smiling at her. He was precious, the best thing she'd ever done.

She'd get through this blip in life and go on from there.

Taking the turn into the lane for the Barton Inn, she admired the addition Chelsea and Jack had just had put on the house now that there were more people living there. It had been a smart decision.

With no guests for the weekend, she would get a guest room tonight, then move to their side of the house for the days leading up to New Year's Eve, if she chose to stay. They were having a huge New Year's Eve party and were fully booked as of the moment.

She had been excited when her brother told her they were adding cabins because business was booming; that would be one less thing she had to find for wedding guests. In a town as small as this one, hotel accommodations could be scarce.

Pulling up to the house where she'd grown up, she pulled into the guest lot on the side just as the sky began to darken. Every light in the house was on, it looked like. The windows were festooned with wreaths with twinkling lights and red ribbons. Chelsea and the inn manager, Adele, had really outdone themselves. The snow was only supposed to accumulate to about three inches, not so much that people couldn't get around.

She honked her horn and waited for Jack to come out to help her inside. Instead of just Jack, she got the whole household, as well as one guy she remembered from the wedding last weekend.

Chelsea and Jack each hugged her. Jack kissed her crown, then immediately turned to fight over who got to take the baby into the house. Adele hugged Paige, then grabbed the bags out of the front seat while directing Frank, the cook, and the guy she called Logan and introduced as her boyfriend, to start unloading the trunk. Frank kissed her on the cheek and Logan shook hands with her before both loaded up their big arms and headed into the house. She took the box of presents from the trunk, and that was everything. That was a hell of a lot quicker than she had expected.

She stood in the driveway for just a minute, breathing in the country air and preparing herself for the chaos that would be the Barton Inn with all these people here. She'd grown accustomed to quiet, with just her and Ian. There would be little of that with Mazzy, her niece, running around and demanding to hold Ian, Frank asking what she wanted to eat since she didn't eat enough, Chelsea and Jack making sure she was comfortable, and Adele asking the same thing. And then in about two hours the real party would start, and they should have even more guests—Nate and Claudia with their son, May and Brad and their daughter, Dex and Zoe, and Dex's brother and his young family. The house was going to be full to the rafters. But she wouldn't trade it for the world, especially since she'd be able to go home tonight with a full belly, a happy mind, good conversation, and sleep peacefully in her own apartment if she wanted.

She entered the house, set the box of presents near the tree in the living room, and went to find her son. He was safely ensconced in Mazzy's arms, with Chelsea sitting next to them, talking to him as if he understood. Maybe he did. A smile popped out on his little face and filled Paige's heart with so much love she paused to soak in the feeling that everything was going to be all right. She might not have the circumstances she had expected at one time, but she had an amazing family, awesome friends, and a support network anyone would be blessed to have. She could have asked for more, but she was happy with what she had.

She left the downstairs and went up to her room. She wouldn't be getting her son back any time soon; that was a given the second she stepped foot in the house. The break was welcome. Being the sole caregiver could be wearying.

So she'd take a few moments to herself, freshen up, then go back downstairs to see if she could help with prep for the big party tonight. Surely there was something she could do in the kitchen with Frank, to take her mind off the disappointment she was still fighting, that Mason had not called.

Checking her face in the mirror, she put on a little makeup, brushed out her hair, and put on clothes that didn't scream "mom" for the first time in ages, outside of work hours.

She was leaving her room when her cell phone rang from the nightstand next to her bed. She could leave it up here. Everyone important to her was downstairs ready to make merry for Christmas.

She hesitated, though, and caught the phone up only after it had gone to voicemail. Mason. Of course it was. And what would his excuse be? He'd asked for Christmas Day, but she'd shut him down, saying that day was for family only. Had he deliberately skipped yesterday to force her hand for tomorrow?

Tapping the phone against her chin, she debated whether or not to listen to his voicemail. She could ignore it, just answer it the day after Christmas, and fake apologize that she hadn't seen the missed call until then.

But that would only prolong things, and she wasn't

that petty. If she were him, she'd be devastated to the bottom of her very soul that she'd missed out on so much of their little guy's life already. He'd missed the first smile, the first hand waving, the way Ian grabbed on to a person's fingers and wouldn't let go. There was only so much he could do in a restaurant, and she'd deliberately kept the visits on neutral territory because she'd still been hurting.

But that didn't mean she had to hurt him, too.

Dialing into the voicemail box, she went through the motions to get the message. What would he say? She braced herself, just in case he'd decided to walk again and didn't want to have anything to do with them now. It was a worry that constantly sat at the back of her mind.

"Paige, oh man, I am so sorry I missed last night. I was helping Mrs. Treehelm with a cat on her roof, and I swear I fell off the ladder. I broke my arm. Ended up in the damn emergency room but didn't get seen until almost three o'clock in the morning because there was a big accident on the turnpike last night and they had to see those people first. I'm so sorry. I wanted to be there, and now I messed it up. I didn't know if there was some way to reschedule. I have stuff for Ian and don't want to miss out on his first Christmas." His voice got thick at that point, and he cleared his throat before continuing. "Yeah, well, if you can make time, I'd appreciate it. If you can't, then I guess I'll just figure something else out, maybe for another time. I really want—" But the voicemail system must have timed out, because it cut him off.

She sat on the edge of the bed with the phone in her hand. What had he wanted? What did she want?

Flopping back on the bed, she wished she knew both of those wants, and why he made her feel like her whole life was a maelstrom every time he came around.

Chapter Two

In all the time he and Paige had been together, she'd never introduced him to her family. Mason only knew where the Barton Inn was because a buddy of his had gone to a wedding there a month or so ago and had been able to give him directions.

Directions he hadn't been able to use the other day because of that stupid fall. He was happy to help his neighbor, but why on that day, with those results? Lately he felt like his whole life was either a comedy of errors or a drama of comic proportions.

He had a GPS, but he was too nervous to focus on it. Instead he memorized the directions and then recited them to himself over and over as he made his way to Christmas Eve at the inn. When he'd left that message for Paige, he'd been almost positive he wouldn't hear from her until after New Year's. A part of him knew he would have deserved it, accident or not. But she had called. And though she sounded a bit stiff, it wasn't the downright chill of their first few conversations after his return to town.

He would have preferred to just have a visit at Paige's townhouse, but she had insisted on neutral territory, and this was as neutral as they got, unless he wanted to go to yet another restaurant and have a stilted dinner with her whole family in attendance.

He flipped down the visor as he made the last turn

before the inn. The sun flashed in his eyes anyway as it lowered. They had originally scheduled a full three hours yesterday, and he hadn't asked if that had changed for tonight. From the way she'd talked, he had a feeling the crowd was going to be bigger than just her brother, sister-in-law, and niece. He was going to have to make do. He was the one who had left, not without reason, but he'd left. He'd tried calling her, but he figured at that point she was probably so pissed at him that he could have sent a skywriter and she would have found some way to make it rain.

At least maybe this time he could hold Ian, since she wouldn't insist he was fine in his car seat and didn't need to be interrupted or he might cry and she didn't want to deal with that in a restaurant.

He'd loved Paige, but she had always been difficult and demanding and in control. While initially he had invited the challenge of making her lose control, the aftermath of their breakup had been anything but good. And while most of it was his fault, she had never tried to meet him halfway.

And he'd better start thinking better thoughts, ones just about his little guy, or he'd go into this first Christmas with an attitude he couldn't afford with so many people waiting for him to make a mistake.

The house was beautiful. Paige had told him once that she'd grown up here, and he could see why she had loved it. With the wide front porch, the bay windows, and the surrounding land, this must have been quite the place for her and her brother to run around when they were younger. A tire swing hung from a big oak tree to the left of the driveway as he made his way around the side. Paige had told him where to park and when to arrive. He couldn't help it if he'd gotten here a little faster than he had anticipated. He'd knock on the door, and if they didn't let him in until the appointed time, he'd just wait out in his car with his music station and the bottle of water he'd brought to keep himself hydrated.

Further instructions from Paige had been sent via email. He was to knock on the side door of the inn and wait until someone came to let him in.

He knocked once and stood back. After two minutes, he tried again. Running feet echoed behind the closed door and sounded like a herd of elephants. The door was yanked open, and Chelsea stood with her hand on Mazzy's chest. "Mason."

At least she was friendly. She'd been friendly since the beginning of this whole fiasco of a plan, and he appreciated that. Jack had not been so friendly, and Paige was downright hostile. He didn't mistake the friendliness for having Chelsea on his side, though. He wasn't that stupid. No one was on his side. Except maybe Mazzy, who was more neutral than anything and about as cute a kid as he'd ever met.

"Mason!" she squealed. She seemed to squeal a lot.

"Hi, Mazzy, Chelsea. I know I'm early. The roads weren't as busy as I expected. I can hang out in my car until the appointed time, if you'd rather."

Chelsea stared at him. So did Mazzy. Mazzy's smile told him she was happy to see him, but Chelsea was not as readable. Paige had talked a lot about her best friend from childhood, but he'd never met the woman until a few weeks ago when he'd pressed for some sort of visitation with his son.

A long moment passed. Or maybe it just felt long

since Mazzy was chattering away about a pony she wanted for Christmas and Chelsea had yet to say anything else.

"Come on in. We're just getting set up. Can I get you something to drink?"

Part of him wanted a tall glass of something alcoholic, but he had to be on his best behavior if he expected to ever see Ian more often than just during fully and over-supervised visits.

"A soda would be great, if it's not too much trouble."

"Of course not. Go on into the sitting room. I'll be in soon. Mazzy, why don't you go with Mason?"

"Yep, Mommylove."

He followed the little girl through a hallway and then into the sitting room. A large Christmas tree was decorated with blues and whites, reds and greens. Ornaments hung precisely around the tree with twinkling lights placed at regular intervals.

"This is our form tree. The real fun tree is in our house," Mazzy announced.

Before he was forced to respond, Chelsea came in bearing a glass of soda. "What she means in that this is the formal tree for the inn. We recently had an addition put on the house, and that's where we have the tree with all Mazzy's ornaments and Jack's childhood things."

"Understood. It's beautiful. And you look just as beautiful, Mazzy." He took the glass Chelsea offered as Mazzy twirled back and forth singing some song about the word pretty. He sipped the drink to keep himself from saying anything about wishing he could see the less formal tree. Hell, he wished for a lot of things, but he had to settle for what he could get, at this point.

"Have a seat." Chelsea gestured to a wingback chair.

As soon as he did, Mazzy clambered into his lap, lying on her back with her head on one armrest and her feet dangling over the other.

"She's not shy, sorry," Chelsea said, not looking sorry at all but more indulgent for her outgoing daughter. "Now that she knows your name, you pretty much belong to her." Chelsea chose a chair across from him.

"It's fine. Good practice."

"Right."

Again, with that one word he simply couldn't read her. Mazzy squirmed around in his lap, but didn't say anything else. He wasn't sure what topic would be safe with Chelsea until everybody else showed up. He didn't hear any sounds of people elsewhere, but he supposed activities could be going on in other parts of the house and the noise just didn't reach him.

Chelsea took a sip of her drink and stared at him. He tried not to fidget, but it was not easy.

"Why are you here, Mason?" she asked finally.

And there was the question. Paige had asked a form of it when he'd first gotten her finally to answer his calls and emails and texts. He told Chelsea the same thing he'd told Paige. It wasn't the whole story, but it was the important part. The rest sounded like excuses that he wasn't going to put out there to be judged on. "I want to be a part of Ian's life."

"Why now?"

"He's still young. I'd like him to know who his dad is even if I can't be a day-to-day part of his life."

She peered at him again, waiting for something

more, probably. But he wasn't giving it up. He didn't know how much Paige had told them, and telling their private issues would not get him into her good graces.

Fortunately, Jack came in at that moment. Without a second's hesitation, Mazzy jumped off Mason's lap and ran to her dad, who caught her up and rubbed noses with her. Mason rose from his chair and waited for the brushing of noses to be done before approaching Paige's older brother. He didn't need the man to like him; he simply needed him to not interfere. But not having him hate him would help, too.

"Jack, how are you?" Mason reached out his hand to shake Jack's.

The other man gave him a look similar to Chelsea's, and Mason endured it. Finally Jack took his hand and shook. "Fine, thanks. You're here early."

"The roads weren't as busy as he'd thought," Chelsea piped in, also rising from her chair. She went to stand with her husband and daughter. The wall they built at the entrance to the rest of the house was not lost on Mason.

"Someone's hungry," Paige sang from somewhere behind that wall. She broke through it and entered the room.

Even though their son was only a few months old, she was almost back to the Paige he'd known before. He wished he had been able to see her pregnant, but she'd blocked him from all social media shortly after telling him they were going to be parents.

Now, she was rounder in areas, softer in areas, which he appreciated, not that she was any softer toward him emotionally. She had always been a stunning woman, with her dark brown hair and porcelain skin and those deep blue eyes, but something about motherhood had made her glow even after the birth.

She came to a full stop with Ian in her arms, and the smile faltered on her lips before she forced it back up. "I thought we said five." She glanced pointedly at the grandfather clock to her right. "It's four-fifteen."

No one piped up this time.

"Yes. I overestimated the amount of traffic I might hit and got here early. Chelsea and Mazzy have kept me company so I didn't have to sit out in my car."

She looked him over from head to toe. "I'm going to feed Ian before everyone else gets here. I don't know if you have presents, but if you do, you should go get them now before the house is full. That way we don't waste any of your time."

"Okay, I'll be right back." He made his way through the Barton wall and walked down the hallway to the side door. Every step felt like he was avoiding all the eggshells that seemed to be broken on the floor around him.

He would give her that she had a right to be angry. He'd thought staying acquiescent would make it easier with time. But not telling her what happened, not demanding that she talk with him, keeping his mouth shut, might have been the wrong way to go about this. How did he start the conversation, though? Maybe he should wait until after the holidays, until she could give him an opportunity to be only with her and Ian to explain.

He'd grown up living with his grandmother after his parents had both decided their remote village was too small for their big dreams and left the little town in

Alaska. Their plane went down in a snowstorm on their escape to Juneau, and they had never come back.

Even if he and Paige couldn't work things out, it was important to Mason for Ian to know that his dad wanted him, too, and had not abandoned him just because he'd been taken off guard eleven months ago.

Chapter Three

"You know, if you want things to go well, you might want to ease up on him, Paige." Jack stood in the doorway to the kitchen while Paige grabbed a packet of breast milk from the fridge and warmed it up.

"I thought we agreed you would stay out of this." She kept her back to him, not wanting to see his face.

"Yeah, well, there's staying out and then there's watching you being unbendable."

"And do I have something to be all sunny and funny about?" Seeing Mason standing in her childhood home, looking uncertain and still as handsome as when she met him, had hit her hard in the stomach and the heart. She was still reeling and didn't need her brother to make her feel guilty.

"Yeah, I think you do. At least he wants to be a part of Ian's life."

Paige blew out a breath. Of course he'd go for that one, since Mazzy's father had nothing to do with her. But this wasn't the same thing. Mason had chosen to not be a part from the beginning. He'd stared at her in shock when she'd shown him the pregnancy test and then had walked away without a word.

"You're right, and I'm trying, but there's so much running through my head right now that I don't know what to do."

Her brother's arm came around her from behind.

He rested his chin on her head as he hugged her. "I'm sorry, honey. I know this is hard for you, but maybe it's good to let him in. He seems like an okay guy. I don't know why you never brought him around before, but that's in the past. Now you have Ian *and* us. I think Mason needs you guys. I'm not saying you have to take him back, but at least let him in."

"I'm trying."

"And that's all you can do. Chelsea and I are here for you, no matter what."

She patted his hands, then squeezed them. "I know, and I can't tell you how much I appreciate that."

"Just don't forget it."

"I won't." She stepped out of his embrace to pull the bag from the pot of hot water and position it in a bottle. "You've got my back. I'll never forget that. I just need to figure out what to do with my heart."

Jack left the room after kissing her on the forehead. Paige leaned her head against the fridge. What was she supposed to do? He left when she was three months pregnant and showed back up when Ian was three months old. Okay, so he had called for months before that and had texted her and emailed her. But she could do this alone and didn't need him hovering. Look at Chelsea and Claudia. They'd both managed to raise kids without a man. She could do this.

But did she want to?

Of course, she was choosing to ignore the fact that both those women had steady men in their lives now and were much happier being with the loves of their lives…

Hell, she didn't even know if Mason was only really here for access to Ian. He might think he could do it without her, too, and she was spinning fantasies out of thin air.

Walking back into the sitting room, she came face to face with a mound of wrapped things, both small and big...and extra big. Mazzy was almost vibrating off the floor with excitement, and even Ian had a smile on his face. Chelsea still had him in her arms, but he found her with his eyes when she walked into the room.

Before she could stop herself, she laughed. "What on earth is all this? Did you buy out the toy store or what? Man, Mazzy, I hope Santa got all his shopping done before Mason hit the stores."

Mazzy turned, shaking her finger. "Santa doesn't buy his toys, he makes them all. And this is so cool! I could jump in like a pile of leafs..." She sent a sly look toward Chelsea, but it was Jack who grabbed her off the ground and tickled her.

"We are going to sit here and pretend to be on our good behavior, Mazzy." He rubbed noses with her. "Mason is our guest, and we have to be good. These are for Ian, remember. This is Ian's early Christmas. Ours is tomorrow."

"Oh, no," Mason said, kneeling and placing the last few presents in his arms under the tree. "I brought things for Mazzy, too. I wouldn't dream of making her sit through Christmas for someone else." His eyes got that faraway look in them for just an instant. She'd noticed it before, when they'd dated, but had never been able to pinpoint why it happened. She'd tried to find a pattern of when, yet had never been able to come up with one.

"You didn't have to," Chelsea said.

"I appreciate you opening your home to me. I

wanted to do it."

Mazzy clapped and chortled in Jack's arms. She was going to be beside herself on Christmas morning.

"She can start, if she wants to." He stood with two gifts in his strong hands. He handed one to Mazzy and the other to Paige. "This is for Ian."

He smiled, but it was tentative, like he didn't know if he was supposed to smile at her. Dammit, this was awkward. She needed to break this wall of ice between them if she wanted things to work out for all three of them.

She was convinced now that he wasn't going anywhere. It was time to try to bridge that gap. "Thanks."

The first couple of things were rattles and teething rings and soft cloth blocks. She thanked him, trying to picture where she was going to put all this stuff in her townhouse.

Mazzy was having a blast opening baby dolls and a miniature tea set, a bear that went with the tea set, and a house for the bear.

He kept coming with the gifts, and they moved into clothes and blankets and hooded towels, more clothes, tiny socks, a bathtub, diapers, an umbrella stroller. The list went on. She was afraid of the huge present he had at the side of the tree. When he brought it over to her, it ended up being a huge polar bear, over five feet tall. At this point she was laughing.

"This is like Christmas and both of my baby showers all wrapped into one. How did you fit all this in your car?"

"Tetris moves. I've still got them." He laughed too, and his shining eyes made her stutter.

"Well, um, thanks."

"Thank you, Mason! I love it all. All of it! So many cool stuffs!" Mazzy hugged his legs, and he reached down to pat her shoulder.

"I'm glad, sugar. Now are you ready to watch everyone else open their gifts? Can you help me hand them out? You'll be like a Santa's elf in training."

The little girl's eyes gleamed, and she clapped her hands.

"Oh." Chelsea said, looking over at Jack with a helpless expression.

Mason couldn't be oblivious to the exchange, but he pretended to be as he smiled at Mazzy and handed her the first gift for Chelsea. Next he had one for Jack, and then there were three for her.

She hadn't gotten him anything.

Chelsea exclaimed in glee over the handprinted scarf in bold watercolors, immediately wrapping it around her neck. Jack's gift was a set of custom-made shot glasses with the inn's logo on them. She was almost afraid to see what her gifts were.

Mazzy delivered one final gift to her mom.

"That's for your whole family," Mason said from his post by the Christmas tree.

It was a huge box. Mazzy helped pull the paper off, Jack cracked open the tape on the plain brown box, and Chelsea pulled out handfuls of tissue paper. They worked like a team in the best possible way. Jack pulled out a wicker basket with hinges. Rising from her chair, Chelsea handed Ian to Paige and then sat back down for Jack to place the basket in her lap. With Mazzy perched on the arm of the chair, Chelsea lifted the lid. Paige couldn't see what it was from her chair, but the gasp from the two females was enough to make her curiosity too much for her to remain sitting.

Getting up from her chair, she placed her three gifts on the floor and came around to their group. Inside the basket was a beautiful picnic set complete with tablecloth, wine glasses etched with a tree, and The Barton Family in a scrolling script. Mazzy had her own plastic cup in a riot of colors. The dishes were plastic but reminded Paige of peacocks with the many deep jewel-toned colors. He couldn't have picked a better gift for a family who loved to explore nature and just be together.

Was she ready for what he'd bought for her?

Backing away from the trio, she walked straight over to Mason and handed their son to him. After a moment in which shock and a bit of fright raced across his face, Mason held on tight to the little bundle.

"He's not a big squirmer, but sometimes he will try to wiggle away. If you keep his head in the crook of your arm, he should settle right in." She remained where she was for a moment, just long enough to make sure Mason relaxed back into his chair, and then she trusted that she knew what she was doing.

Going back to her chair, she picked her three gifts off the floor and arranged them in her lap. "You didn't have to do this."

He didn't look up from their son. Mason's eyes roamed over the boy, the fingers of his right hand picking up tiny fingers, smoothing over the light brown eyebrows that were just coming in, ruffling through the sparse hair on Ian's head. "I know, Paige. I wanted to." Now he did look up at her. "Nothing in that wrapping will ever compare to what you just did for me. Thank you." His gaze dropped back to Ian, and a smile spread across both their faces.

Since the moment Ian had come into the world hollering, she hadn't been able to deny he looked like Mason. The almost-black hair, the olive-toned skin, the brown eyes. And when they smiled at each other, even the crook of their lips was similar.

She silently let out the breath she'd been holding. Chelsea caught her eye and gave her an encouraging smile. This did not mean they were getting back together, but it sure would be easier to be on the same side.

And then she opened her gift—and tried with everything she had to keep the tears in check. Instead she laughed long and loud. Both Ian and Mason looked at her, along with Jack and Chelsea. From the wrapping paper, she pulled a single disc. In Mason's neat scrawl were the words Wedding Planner Extraordinaire and Super Mom.

"You didn't."

"I finished it three weeks ago but wanted to wait to give it to you."

"What is it?" Chelsea asked, moving across the room to stand behind Paige's shoulder.

"It's a computer program Mason was working on right after we started dating. It's a huge organizer with all the things I could possibly need for my business." She looked at him to find him smiling at her. "Do I assume the Mom thing is an add-on?"

"I figured it couldn't hurt to have that as a separate file. And it's also an app that you can install on your phone if you want."

Maybe this wasn't holding her son for the first

time, but it was a close second. As a successful computer programmer, he didn't have a ton of free time, she knew, and when he'd started on this project so many months ago, he'd told her it would take a while due to the complexity of everything she wanted in it.

And he'd worked on it, continued to work on it through the months when they didn't talk, through her constant dismissal of his phone calls. Through the rough visits in restaurants where she refused to let him hold his son, through the hoops she'd made him jump and the crumbs she'd given him when she'd never let him explain himself, even when he tried to get a word in.

"Jack, Chelsea, would you mind stepping out for a few minutes?" She locked gazes with Mason.

Not two seconds passed before they were shepherding Mazzy out of the room. The little girl was protesting because Paige hadn't asked her to leave, only Mommylove and Daddylove. Paige laughed, a sound that seemed to unfurl the cocoon her heart had been sleeping in.

"Dare I open these two other gifts?" she said, smiling for the first time in his presence without having to force it.

"Go ahead."

She unwrapped the first one. A beautiful polar bear carved from some material with a high polish. "Do I sense a theme? This is beautiful, but I don't remember you liking polar bears that much."

He paused. He seemed to want to say something else but halted with his lips parted.

"Say it. Whatever it is, say it."

"I didn't want to leave."

Chapter Four

The smile that had been on her face winked out, replaced with flattened lips. She'd said to say it, and Mason was going to now even if it made things more difficult.

"Hear me out."

She nodded, but it was a tight gesture, and her hands clenched over the top of the figurine he'd spent hours carving out of a caribou antler.

"I didn't want to leave. I've been trying to come up with a way to tell you what happened without it sounding like excuses. I haven't figured it out yet, so I'm just going to tell you before you open the next gift."

He waited a moment to see if she'd tell him to stop or that she didn't want to hear what he had to say, but she continued to sit there.

"I've been in Alaska."

"What?"

Her high-pitched squawk made Ian jerk in Mason's arms. He patted the little boy's belly to calm him. It worked, and he went back to sucking his fist.

"I've been in Alaska. After you told me about the pregnancy, I did need some time to think about things, not to get away from you but to consider if it would be a good idea to ask you to marry me or if you'd be angry because we hadn't talked about getting married before and I didn't want you to think that was the only reason I would want to marry you. And I wasn't expecting to hear I was going to be a father. You took me completely off guard and then got pissed when I didn't leap with joy immediately. I felt bad and took the time, thinking I had more, to get things right and then come back to you."

He checked her expression. Nothing he'd said yet had unflattened her lips. He had to forge ahead.

"Then my grandmother got sick. I got the call from my grandmother's neighbor. They live out in the wilds of Alaska, and it's fifty miles to the nearest area for cell service. He called to say Nana had fallen and was refusing to be taken to a hospital. She's old school. She would have lived in an igloo if she could. Instead, she had a small house on a hill, and that's where I was raised. She did her best after my parents died, but she liked the old ways and herbal medicine. I flew out the week after you told me. I tried to call, but you didn't answer, and I wasn't going to leave a message. I kept thinking I'd have time to get back to you, but then I took a small plane to my grandmother and sat by her side for six months while the healers came and went. I carved that piece in your hand every day while I worried about her. I tried to get a call through to you a couple times, but they kept dropping."

He was babbling, and she was probably only getting every third word, with all the information he was bombarding her with, but it was all true. It sounded like some fantastic, wild story, but every word was truth. In the five months they'd been together, their relationship had been very much on the surface. They'd gone out on dates, had fun, talked about current events, her work, his, but hadn't gotten very far in the relationship part because they'd both had past relationships that had gone too fast. They'd taken it slow together, and then they'd created a child, and he'd wrecked everything by not being here.

But he couldn't have done anything different.

"All I can say is I'm sorry. Nothing turned out the way I thought it would, and now I feel like we're starting from scratch, but I'd like to know if we might have a chance. I know I messed up. I really do, but I can't help but wish you'd believe me and let us see if we can make a family before we throw it all away."

A single tear trailed down her cheek. Was she angry? God, would she just say something? Anything? He wanted to go to her, but he was afraid to move off the chair with Ian in his arms. What if he dropped him?

"Can you please come over here? I don't want to jostle Ian or I'd be over there already."

As if in slow motion, she rose from her chair and made her way to him. She crouched at his knee.

"I don't even know where to start." She swiped at the tear in her eye.

"I didn't know how to finish."

"We're a pair," she said on a laugh. "I didn't answer your calls because I was trying to punish you for not coming back soon enough, and you had your grandmother to worry about. Then I refused to let anyone tell you I had to be on bed rest for the last three months of the pregnancy."

"Oh, Paige, I'm so sorry."

"No, don't be. No one was blameless here, but no one was to blame, either. Maybe we just didn't trust each other enough." She gripped his knee harder.

"I'd like to change that. Scratch that. I want to

change that." He leaned forward, making sure to keep a firm hand on their son.

She met him halfway with a kiss that melted the rest of the ice that had encased his heart as he'd flown away from her. Now that he was back, he wanted to know everything. He didn't think he could take it slow this time, but they'd talk about that later. Right now, he had his family in his arms, and he couldn't ask for anything more.

Chapter Five

Paige left her guys in the sitting room while she went to get a glass of water and a box of tissues. Chelsea and Frank were both in the kitchen when she arrived. She wasn't overly surprised.

"So?" Chelsea said, hope shining in her eyes.

Paige knew she had been wondering for months if Paige was going to be able to survive this on her own. For Paige's part, she knew she could have, but she'd rather not do it alone if all she had to do was unbend enough to meet Mason halfway.

"We're going to try again. A lot happened. I'll tell you all about it tomorrow. Right now I want to get back to my guys."

"Your guys, huh?" Frank said with a satisfied smile on his lips.

She smiled. "Yep, my guys." She turned back to Chelsea. "Is it okay if Mason stays the night tonight? We'll be in separate rooms, but I'd like him to be here for Christmas morning, if that's okay."

Chelsea grabbed her up in a hug. "That's a ridiculous question. Of course he can stay. Are you sure you'd rather not go back to your townhouse so you can have privacy?"

"I'm positive. I think we need this, and I don't want to miss the party tonight. I want to introduce him to everyone and get the ball rolling for us to be a family."

Chelsea's eyes glassed up, and she could almost swear Frank's did too.

"Oh, honey. I'm so happy for you guys, and Jack is going to be thrilled. He's been so worried about you."

Paige laughed around the lump in her throat. "Tell him to stop worrying. I was fine before, but I'm even better now. I love you guys." A group hug ensued, and then the side doorbell rang.

Frank looked at the clock on the wall. "Guests arriving. I'd better get these snacks out or the guys are going to have a fit. They come here for my snacks, you know."

Paige and Chelsea laughed.

"Get back to the sitting room," Chelsea said. "Close the pocket doors and you can have a few more minutes of privacy before the whole party descends on you."

"Yes, ma'am."

Swatting at her arm, Chelsea shooed her out of the kitchen. Paige went without protest.

She found Ian sleeping in his father's arms, his fingers curled around Mason's index finger.

"It's magic, isn't it?" she asked quietly.

Mason looked up at her with tears in his eyes. "Thank you for him. Thank you for you. Thank you for giving us another chance. Maybe this time we'll get it right."

"We will, Mason. We'll get it right this time. I promise."

"You should open your other present."

She'd completely forgotten about the last present. Grabbing it off the table next to her chair, she perched on the arm of his chair. Slowly she unwrapped the present, not sure what to expect.

A crystal heart lay nestled in a blue velvet-lined box. Etched in the glass was her favorite line from a movie. "As you wish."

She leaned over and kissed him full on the mouth. "I'm going to hold you to that." She laughed.

"As long as you hold me, that's all I need."

Chapter Six

The party was in full swing. Everyone had their significant others and children with them. The house was full, bellies were stuffed, and merriment filled the air. Frank stood back in the foyer and watched his friends—no, his family—enjoy one another. Kids played with each other, with Justin riding herd over all the little ones. Paige hadn't stopped touching Mason, who hadn't let anyone hold that precious boy of theirs, not even Frank. He'd have to remedy that soon. Eventually he'd catch them in a moment and use it to his advantage. He had put mistletoe in the doorways of each room. Eventually they would break away from everyone congratulating them long enough to steal a kiss or two, and then he'd steal that baby.

Mazzy ran up to him, swung a time of two off his arm, and dashed away. He was not looking forward to that one growing up. She was already a handful and would probably be more than that as a teenager. But they had years until that, and she had two strong parents. In the meantime, those two had an announcement of their own they would probably be making later this evening. An announcement that would make the addition even more important because they'd have a nursery to decorate.

Nate and Claudia laughed over in the corner about something Zoe said. He was happy to see those four paired off right, too. Dex had done some work for him recently to clear up a couple of things from his past, and now he was looking forward to moving along with his own life. In fact, he hoped to maybe use some of the mistletoe himself before Santa came down the chimney.

Delly and Ethan sat near the fireplace holding hands, while Justin carried Phoebe around to show her all the ornaments on the tree in the sitting room. Brad and May sat near them with Lucy sprawled across their laps. Sam stood with his arm around Jocelyn. What a lady that one was. Sam deserved all the happiness he could get. He knew what the fellow military man had gone through and how it could rip you apart. But Sam was getting his second chance. Frank had made sure to pull him aside the other day, though, and let him know that if he ever needed someone to talk to there was a bunch of ex-navy guys who got together for poker a few times a month. Sam had gripped his hand and thanked him. Frank brushed it off. He'd been there and done that.

He looked around for the butterfly who constantly flitted around this house, the glue he both admired and loved like a daughter. Adele had finally found a chair, or really more of a lap, since Logan had pulled her down to sit on him instead of letting her have the spot next to him. Now that one he hadn't seen coming, but he was sure glad they'd managed to not be idiots about realizing they belonged together. He saw great things for them, especially once those cabins were built and the two of them ran them. Logan would still be doing the construction thing and Adele was more than capable of keeping the cabins in line, but they each complemented the other enough to work well as a team.

He couldn't wait for their kids to come along. He'd have to for a little bit, though, since they should probably get married first. But he wanted those red-haired cuties running around before too much longer.

Finally, he saw his chance. Mason went to hand the kid off to Chelsea so he could accept a gift from Paige. Frank intercepted the pass like the ex-football player he was, and laughed as he double-timed it out of the room to answer the door.

He really hoped it was the last guest. He'd been looking forward to seeing this person for days now.

He pulled the door open, knowing full well there was a ball of mistletoe right above the woman's head. He looked up, and so did she.

Her laugh was contagious. "I probably shouldn't be here, and it would be bad form for the kids to see me for the first time here kissing you. I didn't even tell my daughter I'd been invited."

"Pssh. They're all so googly-eyed over their other half they'll probably never notice."

She kissed him on his lips, just a soft brush that made the newly shaved hairs on the back of his neck stand up. "Whew!"

"I'm flexible too," she said, slyly, sashaying past him and into the party before he could introduce her as his date for the night.

He looked down into the sleepy eyes of his partner in crime. "Whoo-wee, Ian, I think I might have my hands full with that woman. I have to tell you, I'm very much looking forward to that."

Ian laughed and waved his hands in the air.

"I agree. Cheering is about what every nerve ending in my body is doing as I watch Flo Caster walk down the hall in those heels."

The woman in question looked back over her bare shoulder and blew him a kiss before she entered the fray.

He'd used the mistletoe once, but next time his hands were going to be free and he'd show her he knew exactly what to do with flexible…

A word about the author...

Misty Simon loves a good story and decided one day that she would try her hand at it. Eventually she got it right. There's nothing better in the world than making someone laugh, and she hopes everyone at least snickers in the right places when reading her books.

She lives with her husband, daughter, and three insane dogs in Central Pennsylvania, where she is hard at work on her next novel or three. She loves to hear from readers so drop her a line at:

misty@mistysimon.com
www.mistysimon.com

www.ingramcontent.com/pod-product-compliance
Lightning Source LLC
Chambersburg PA
CBHW060934180626
46817CB00004B/1529